A Lady In Full Bloom

THE DARROW SISTERS
BOOK THREE

FIONA MIERS

Chapter One

Mary stood before the full-length mirror in her bedroom, twirling from side to side. Her gown draped her in luminous pale blue silk, shimmering in the soft candlelight. She veered from pure excitement to raw nerves, the fluttering of butterflies in her stomach flowing from one extreme to the other in a continuous cycle.

It was the first ball of the season, as well as her debutante ball. The night had finally arrived after months of preparation and countless fittings for a wardrobe of gowns fit for a princess.

Her maid, Emily, pulled the chintz chair from the dressing table. "Time to do your hair, Miss Mary."

"As long as you don't poke and prod at my head." Mary sighed and flopped onto the seat. "The ball hasn't even started yet, and I'm exhausted just from getting ready."

"You weren't planning to attend in one of your cotton gardening dresses, were you? I've heard that if beauty doesn't hurt, you aren't trying hard enough."

"I'm not keen on suffering just to look good." Mary pulled a face of mock horror and lifted her hands to protect her head.

"Just pretend you're pruning the roses. I haven't heard you

complaining about vicious thorns, and I've seen the deep scratches on your arms."

"I complain, Emily, you just aren't in the garden to hear me. Sometimes I even curse."

The maid scoffed. But little did she know, Mary had learned a juicy catalogue of words to express her annoyance and frustration. Not that she would let any of her sisters hear her *confound, drat,* or *blast* any thorn that dared to pierce her skin.

While Mary hummed to herself, Emily swept her coffee-coloured curls up into an elegant coiffure. She pulled a few tendrils free to frame Mary's face. "Almost ready for the event."

"You have quite the talent for arranging hair, Emily. I don't know what I'd do without you." Mary smiled at Emily through the looking glass.

Emily laughed. "Be seen in public with your plaited hair hanging down your back, no doubt."

Mary just shook her head. Some ladies in her position would chastise their maid for such forwardness. But Emily knew when to stay quiet and knew when to make Mary smile.

Mary huffed out a sigh. The weight of duty pressed on Mary's slim shoulders, tempering her excitement. The Darrow family could not afford to be associated with any further scandal. Her father's death, leaving behind unpayable gambling debts, had been disgrace enough. But then came her older sister's rather rushed marriage.

Mary stifled a giggle with her hand. Eleanor had wed Lord Alexander Weston after being caught in the garden like some common doxy. At least Alexander was right behind a hasty wedding, his adoration of Eleanor obvious. Olivia had sidestepped convention by becoming governess and companion to the Duke of Wallingford's young daughter. But she'd returned home in a delicate condition and a cloud of worry before the duke persuaded her to marry him. Thank goodness her condition hadn't been obvious before the wedding.

Her youngest sister, Caroline, had so far escaped notice, but now it was Mary's turn in the unforgiving spotlight of the season. Half of London was no doubt taking bets on when she would stumble.

The family had even embraced their father's illegitimate child into their fold, a most unconventional act among the ton. She didn't regret it. Caleb made a great addition to the family. So far, Lord Weston's position and wealth had shielded the Darrow sisters from the full brunt of society's censure.

Mary clenched her fists, nails biting into her palms. The Darrow family name—what was left of it—rested on her shoulders now, and Mary could not and would not jeopardize their precarious social standing.

Emily finished with her hair and face and startled Mary from her thoughts.

"You look stunning, Miss Mary." Emily grinned as she stepped back to admire her handiwork.

"Thank you, Emily." Mary patted her coiffure. "I feel as if I'm in a dream."

Eleanor entered the room, dressed in an elegant gown in a captivating mix of colours. The fabric flowed gracefully, shimmering with a blend of muted purple, delicate pink, and subtle hints of blue and grey. She looked every bit a confident and poised lady of society. "Not a dream, dearest, it's time for you to attend your very first ball of the season. Are you excited?"

"I think I'm excited." Mary laughed. "It's hard to tell. I'm so nervous." She cuddled into Eleanor's comforting and calming embrace.

Eleanor stroked her back gently. "You look so beautiful, Mary. You will be the star of the ball. The marquess himself will no doubt sing your praises, and Lady Carlisle will fall in love with you."

Mary blushed at her sister's praise. "It was kind of Lady Beatrice to secure us invitations to the Carlisle's ball."

"Indeed but expect quite a crush. The Carlisles are known for their splendid soirees."

"And the rich, spiced drinking chocolate on the desert table." Mary giggled. "I'll use my elbows to ensure I get a cup."

"Elbows, Mary? You sound like Caroline."

Mary gave Eleanor a small smile. "I just hope I can live up to everyone's expectations. What if I say something foolish, or trip and fall in the middle of a dance? Everyone will laugh at me."

"Just claim you're performing an avant-garde version, fresh from

France." Eleonor waved her hand in dismissal. "Everyone will hail you as a revolutionary."

"Revolutionary or mad?"

"Why not both? After all, it's the unpredictable girls who are most memorable."

"Yes, but memorable for the wrong reasons!"

"Nonsense. Just enjoy yourself, and if anyone gives you trouble, I will trip them for you."

Mary jammed her hands on her hips. "Eleanor, you are teasing me."

"Of course, I am, dearest." Eleanor took Mary's hands in hers. "It's natural to have such fears, but unnecessary. Didn't our dance instructor declare you to be the outstanding pupil of the year? Just enjoy the evening. Be yourself, and everything will fall into place. Besides, you have a charming je ne sais quoi that will win over every guest."

Mary's shoulders eased somewhat. She glanced out the window, where the setting sun cast a golden glow over their gardens. Blooming flowers wafted their scent through the open window, the fragrance mingling with the heady aroma of anticipation.

"I suppose I should focus on having a good time." Mary's thoughts drifted to the enchanting world of the ball and the evening ahead. "And I will mention my passion for botany if the conversation allows. It's such a large part of who I am."

Eleanor nodded, a knowing smile on her lips. "It is. Let your love for plants shine through. It's what makes you unique, and anyone worth your time will appreciate that about you."

"I wish Olivia and Caroline could be here too."

"It would be most immodest for Olivia to be seen in public now that she is showing." Eleanor hugged her again. "And Caroline is both too young and is loving her stay with Olivia and James, helping with Charlotte."

"Olivia isn't just showing, she's the size of a whale." Mary giggled again. "Perhaps we could call on them this week to tell them all about my first ball."

"I'm sure they would both love that."

A soft knock at the door interrupted Mary's musings. Lady Alice, her cousin by marriage, best friend, and fellow debutante, peeked in with a bright smile.

"My goodness, that gown is perfection." Alice's eyes twinkled with excitement. "The carriage is waiting, and I can hardly contain myself!"

Mary's nerves eased even more at the sight of her friend. "I'm ready, Alice. Let's make this a night to remember."

In the foyer, Lady Beatrice stood with regal poise, her sharp eyes softened as she regarded Mary and Alice. "You are the very picture of grace and elegance this evening. No matter what may happen, carry yourselves with confidence and charm."

She adjusted a loose curl on Mary's coiffure. "Do not allow mere flattery to sway you, my dear. True character reveals itself in actions, not just words. Keep your wits about you and use discretion in choosing your company."

Turning to Alice, she offered a warm smile. "Your vivacity is your greatest asset, Alice. Let your light shine, but do not forget the decorum expected of you. A lady's dignity is her finest jewel."

She clasped her hands together. "I'm so proud of you both. Enjoy the evening, my loves. Dance, laugh, and make the most of what I'm sure will be a splendid occasion."

Lady Beatrice would be following them later, as Alexander would be going back for her. For now, though, she kissed them both on the cheek.

As they made their way to the carriage, Alice chattered about the evening ahead. Mary gave trite answers, her mind elsewhere. After all, Lady Beatrice had just reminded her of the decorum expected of her, and the risk to her family if she failed in the eyes of the ton. Eleanor walked alongside them, her presence a steadying influence.

"You both look like princesses out for a night on the town." Eleanor hugged them both. "Just remember, this is your night. Enjoy every moment."

Alice grinned, linking her arm with Mary's. "We will. And don't worry, I'll make sure Mary doesn't get too lost in her thoughts about plants."

Mary laughed along with them. "I promise I'll try to keep my botanical musings to a minimum."

When they arrived at the Carlisle's grand townhouse, a surge of awe curled within Mary. Dozens of carriages as handsome as Alexander's jostled for position on the street. A warm, inviting glow from hundreds of lanterns illuminated the mansion. The sound of music and laughter already filled the air, the atmosphere electric with the energy of the gathering.

Alexander tapped his walking cane on the roof of the carriage. "We'll get out here, driver."

Mary nodded her agreement. "It's just a short walk to the house, which is better than waiting in this queue of carriages to get closer."

"Remember, Mary," Eleanor whispered as they made their way up the steps. "Just be yourself."

Mary nodded, her heart pounding in her chest. As the doors swung open, and they stepped into the grand foyer, a whirlwind of activity enveloped her. She drifted to the large, impressive bouquets greeting guests at the entrance. But then, the floral garlands and swags draped over doorways, staircases, and along the edges of tables, caught her eye. She squeezed Eleanor's hand. "Are any flowers left in London's flower shops?"

"Possibly not." Eleanor shook her hand free from Mary's grip. "But it's far too early in the evening for you to obsess about flowers."

"Right." Mary nodded as she gazed into the ballroom, its crystal chandeliers casting a dazzling light over a crush of elegantly dressed guests.

Alexander took his leave to return for Lady Beatrice with a saucy kiss right on Eleanor's lips. Mary looked on in longing, so wanting love for herself. Genuine love, like Eleanor and Olivia had found.

Taking a deep breath, Mary allowed herself to be swept up in the evening's excitement. She greeted familiar faces, exchanged pleasantries with acquaintances, and tried her best to remember the names of the many new people to whom she was introduced.

As the evening progressed, Mary's dance card filled. She'd hardly had a moment to herself until she begged off from the last country dance of the set. She could not face another physical workout of skipping, hopping, and brisk walking, not until she had drunk something to quench her thirst, at least.

Mary re-joined Eleanor and Alice at the edge of the ballroom. "I am as parched as a camel in the middle of the Sahara Desert."

"I guessed you might be." Eleanor's eyes sparkled with pride as she handed Mary a glass of punch. "You look radiant, and you danced beautifully. How are you feeling?"

"A little overwhelmed, but I'm enjoying myself." Mary drained the glass of punch. "It's all so much to take in. I'll never remember everyone's names."

"You will. This is only the first ball. There will be so many more to come." Eleanor pressed a fruit tart into Mary's hand. "Eat. If you get tipsy from too much punch and not enough food, we will have to take you home in disgrace."

Alice grinned, giving Mary a playful nudge. "You've danced more than me. I don't know how you are still standing. Maybe you will find a handsome gentleman who shares your love for plants. Wouldn't that be perfect?"

Unlikely though it was, Mary could still dream she'd find the perfect husband during the season. And no matter what, the evening was bound to be memorable. Mary realised that she had not yet responded to Alice.

"Indeed, it would." Mary's smile faltered. "Dearest Alice, I've abandoned you. I'm so sorry."

"Don't be silly." Alice tapped her fan against Mary's gloved arm. "You are one of the beautiful Darrow sisters with an eye-watering dowry, while I'm just poor relation, Miss Alice with not a penny to my name.

"Stop it." Mary tapped Alice with her fan.

"Girls," Eleanor admonished. "We are making a good impression, remember. Alice, come with me. I see the viscount I promised to introduce you to."

Left alone, Mary edged closer to a display of huge ferns. The poor things were unlikely to survive the heat so close to ensconced candles. She caught the eye of one of Lord Weston's friends, and her skin tingled with pleasure when he gave her a nod and approached.

"Good evening, Lady Mary." He bowed, though not low enough

that she couldn't see his gaze twinkling with amusement. "I must say, this handsome fern is doing an excellent job as your chaperone."

"Lord Everhart." She curtsied. "Eleanor isn't far... she just left to... I um... I mean, it's quite a lovely fern, isn't it?"

Heat climbed up her face. Had she ever blurted out such inane drivel before? And in front of the tall, dark, and intriguing Lord Nathaniel Everhart, whom she had secretly crushed on since meeting him at Eleanor's wedding to Alexander. She'd imagined conversations with him in the privacy of her head and her bedroom until almost being caught by her youngest sister, Caroline. None of those conversations had her this tongue-tied, though.

Lord Everhart was polite enough not to notice. "It's not every day one encounters a lady in hiding. May I join you in your leafy refuge?"

"Of course. Though it is a little cramped." Mary moved closer to the fern.

He joined her in the alcove, standing as far as he could from her to maintain a polite distance. His smile widened. "I've always admired ferns, they're so—"

"Green?" Mary finished for him. She felt a strange mix of embarrassment and amusement.

"Quite. So, tell me, do you often take refuge behind foliage at social gatherings?"

Mary grinned at him. "I don't have enough experience to tell. Though I imagine I will, if the company is daunting. This is my first ball, you know."

"Then I consider myself honoured to share this botanical sanctuary with you. Shall we discuss the merits of ferns over, say, roses?"

"Ferns are more reliable than roses, always green and cheerful. Roses, for all their beauty, have thorns, and their beauty is short-lived."

"A wise observation." Lord Everhart's brow furrowed. "Do you find the guests here a thorny as roses?"

Mary giggled. "No, though a few are a little prickly."

Their laughter drew the attention of other guests, but Mary didn't mind one bit.

"Shall we emerge from our leafy haven, Lady Mary? I believe a waltz is about to start, and it would be a shame to let such an enticing evening go to waste."

Mary was about to take Lord Everhart's arm when an older family friend, Lord Satterfield, approached with the handsomest man she had ever seen.

Tall and impeccably dressed, the stranger possessed an air of confident elegance. His blond hair perfectly coiffed, his chiselled features exuding an effortless charm. Eyes the colour of a stormy sea locked onto hers with an intensity that made her breath catch. His smile, slow and deliberate, revealed a hint of mischief as he bowed before her.

"Lady Mary, may I introduce my nephew, Lord Sebastian Blackwood, Earl of Ravenshire," Lord Jonathon announced with a note of pride. "Lord Blackwood, this is Lady Mary Darrow."

"An honour, Lady Mary." Sebastian's voice, smooth and rich as velvet, tickled her ears. "I have heard much about your beauty and grace, but I see now that simple words do you no justice."

A warm flush spread across her cheeks as she dropped into a curtsy, struggling to maintain her composure under his piercing gaze. "You are too kind, Lord Blackwood."

As Nathaniel stepped back, allowing the introduction to take place, the full weight of Sebastian's attention hit Mary. It was both exhilarating and unsettling. She glanced at Nate, his expression unreadable.

"Let us join the dance." Sebastian held out his arm. Nathaniel stepped back further, as if to clear the way for the newcomer, and Mary found herself swept onto the dance floor.

Mary's heart raced as she took Lord Sebastian Blackwood's outstretched hand, her nerves jangling at the prospect of her first waltz in public. The music began, a soft, lilting tune that seemed to float on the air. As Sebastian led her onto the dance floor, she could feel the eyes of the assembled guests upon them, their whispers and glances adding to her anxiety.

Lord Everhart had been about to ask her, she was sure of it, but he stepped back after the introductions. Then Lord Blackwood whisked her onto the dance floor. And like a fresh-from-the-schoolroom debutante, she'd let him. She pushed the thought of dancing with Nate aside, determined to enjoy the evening.

Sebastian placed his hand on her waist, his touch gentle yet firm, and drew her a little closer than was proper. A shiver of uncertainty ran through her, but his confident smile and the effortless grace with which he guided her through the steps eased the tightness between her shoulder blades.

"You dance so well, Lady Mary." Sebastian's soothing murmur was a balm to her frayed nerves. "It's as if you've been waltzing all your life."

Mary managed a shy smile, her earlier discomfort beginning to fade. "Thank you, Lord Blackwood. I must admit, I was quite nervous."

"There is no need for nerves when your steps are perfect." His gaze locked onto hers with an intensity that made her blush. "You are the most enchanting partner I've ever had the pleasure of dancing with."

Despite the closeness of his hold, or perhaps because of it, Mary found herself won over by his charm. He twirled her across the floor, and for a few moments, the magic of the moment swept her away, her earlier worries forgotten in the face of Sebastian's captivating presence.

His compliments flowed, praising her beauty, her grace, even the colour of her gown. Mary grew tongue-tied, unaccustomed to such flattery.

"You are a vision, Lady Mary," Sebastian said, his voice smooth as velvet. "I daresay, the stars themselves pale compared to your radiance tonight."

Mary blushed, struggling to find a suitable response. "You are too kind, my lord. It is a lovely evening, is it not?"

"Indeed, it is." Sebastian's gaze never left hers. "But it is your presence that makes the evening remarkable. Let's do away with the encumbrance of titles, shall we? Mary and Sebastian are so much easy to say."

She blushed again but nodded her agreement. Heavens above, what would Eleanor say if she heard her call Lord Blackwood by his first name?

When the dance ended, Sebastian escorted her back to Eleanor. Mary curtsied, thanking him for the dance, and returned to Eleanor's side.

Eleanor, ever perceptive, raised an eyebrow as she watched the young lord walk away. "He's quite the charmer, isn't he?"

Mary nodded. "He is. Almost too charming. Though he is most respectful as well and a magnificent dancer, I can't help but feel both flattered and confused."

Sebastian's words were complimentary, but they lacked the warmth and genuine interest she had felt in Lord Everhart's company. There was an ease with him, an unspoken understanding that made their conversation flow. Perhaps it was just their shared interest in botany and a recognition that no shallow flattery was needed between them.

Eleanor sighed, glancing around the ballroom. "Appearances can deceive, Mary. Blackwood is a reputed rake for good reason. Just be cautious."

Mary frowned, her gaze following Sebastian as he moved through the crowd. "I'll keep that in mind," she promised, though she found it difficult to reconcile Eleanor's warning with the charming man with whom she had just danced.

Her thoughts drifted back to Lord Everhart, and she looked around, hoping to catch sight of him. But he was no longer at the fern where they had first met. Disappointment settled in her chest. She had so many questions for him, so much she wanted to discuss. His sudden absence left her feeling oddly bereft.

As the evening wore on, Mary danced with so many partners, she could not place names and faces together, yet she enjoyed herself enormously. Eleanor made sure Alice danced almost as often, her friend's bright laughter a constant source of joy for Mary. However, no matter how many times she changed partners, her mind kept wandering back to Nate Everhart.

Chapter Two

Nate stood a few feet away, his eyes narrowing as he watched the exchange between Lady Mary and Blackwood. The interruption was most unwelcome. He should have been more assertive, made his desire to dance with her clear. Unease gnawed at him. Allowing her to dance with that cad was a mistake.

Blackwood's charming smile concealed a heart encased in ice. The man had a history of leaving broken hearts in his wake. His charm and smooth manners posed a threat to any young lady, though he typically preyed upon young widows and bored married women. Whispers in drawing rooms across the country told tales of his exploits, each story more scandalous than the last.

He remembered a summer two years ago when he witnessed firsthand the havoc Sebastian could wreak. Penelope, a young woman he knew, had fallen for the bounder's charms. Infatuated, she'd believed every honeyed word he whispered. But once he'd tired of her, he discarded her without a second thought. Penelope chased after him, heedless of her reputation. Her family had sent her to a country aunt to avoid tarnishing her younger sisters' prospects. He'd never forget the anguish in her eyes.

Sebastian excelled at deception. He was able to feign sincerity better than anyone Nathaniel had ever met. He could convince anyone that his intentions were pure, but Nate saw through his act. A predatory gleam in Sebastian's eyes betrayed his true nature. To him, women were conquests—thrills to be pursued, possessed, and discarded when boredom set in.

With her innocence and trusting nature, Mary would be vulnerable to someone like Sebastian. He would see her enthusiasm for life and bright-eyed wonder as challenges to conquer. He couldn't let Mary suffer the same fate as Penelope. He had to protect her from Sebastian's deceit. But would she believe him if he just blurted out the truth?

The Darrow family had already endured its share of scandal and the scrutinizing eyes of the ton. They couldn't afford another public embarrassment, especially one involving sweet, innocent Mary. Any involvement with Sebastian would lead to gossip and rumours that could ruin her chances of a respectable match.

Nate had known Eleanor for years, and always felt a protective instinct toward the Darrow sisters. But tonight, something deeper stirred within him when he thought of Mary. Her presence was a balm to his soul, her laughter a melody he longed to hear. She had grown into a remarkable young woman, her natural beauty and grace captivating. He'd always admired her intelligence, wit, and gentle spirit, but now there was a spark between them, one he hadn't felt in a long time.

Sebastian leaned in closer to Mary, his smile too wide. Nathaniel's resolve hardened. Mary would not become another conquest for Blackwood. He would protect her, even if it meant confronting the other man.

He turned his gaze away, scanning the room for familiar faces. The ball was in full swing, the grand chandelier casting a warm glow over guests who twirled and laughed in time with the music.

Nate spotted Lord Alexander Weston across the room and navigated through the throng of guests clustered around the edge of the dance floor. Alexander conversed with a group of gentlemen, but his face lit up with a smile when Nathaniel approached.

"Nate, my old friend." Alexander extended his hand. "It's good to see you."

"And you, Alexander," Nate replied with a firm handshake. "The Carlisle ball is quite the success, as usual."

Alexander chuckled. "Indeed. Though I suspect my sister-in-law is feeling some nerves. It's her first ball in her first season, after all."

Nathaniel's gaze flicked back to where Mary stood, now engaged in animated conversation with Blackwood. "She is handling it well, though I have concerns about certain individuals she might encounter."

Alexander followed Nate's gaze. "I share your reservations about Blackwood. He is a womanizer of the worst kind, though I don't recall him ever seducing a debutante as young as Mary."

"He enjoys turning the young ladies' eyes and hearts to him." Nate's jaw tightened. "It's more than that. There's something about his manner that sets me on edge. Mary deserves better than to be another one of his conquests."

"Agreed. She's a bright young woman, though not without her quirks. Did you know she can spend hours in the garden? She even talks to her plants in the conservatory."

"Of course. They appreciate the company and concern." Nate laughed at Alexander's expression.

"I'd forgotten about your own conservatory. Are you still collecting rare specimens?"

"Whenever I can. I've been looking into a botanical expedition in the Caribbean."

Alexander lifted his eyebrows. "Good Lord, that's quite an excursion."

"Safe as long as you sail to avoid hurricane season." Nate stopped as his friend's gaze narrowed. "I'd be better off sharing this information with Lady Mary. I think she would be more appreciative." Nathaniel's expression softened. "We shared a conversation about plants earlier this evening. It's rare to find a young woman so knowledgeable and enthusiastic about botany."

"It's one thing that makes her so special."

Nate's gaze lingered on Mary, who was now laughing at something Sebastian said. "I just hope she sees through his facade before it's too late."

"She's a sensible girl." Alexander placed a reassuring hand on his shoulder. "She's not alone in this, Nate. We'll both monitor her."

Nathaniel nodded, his protective instincts kicking in. He couldn't deny the growing attraction he felt for Mary, but his primary concern was her safety and well-being. She deserved to enjoy her first season without falling prey to Blackwood's false charm.

As the evening progressed, Nate watched Mary from a distance, his gaze never straying far from her. He observed the way she moved with grace and elegance, the genuine smile that lit up her face. She was a breath of fresh air in the stifling atmosphere of the ton, and he couldn't help his attraction to her.

Alexander re-joined him and offered a glass of champagne. "You look like a man with a lot on his mind."

He accepted the champagne with a grateful nod. "Keeping a watchful eye, that's all."

Alexander chuckled. "Ever the protector, an admirable trait."

Nate sipped his champagne, his gaze drifting back to Mary. "She's special, Alexander. She deserves the chance to enjoy her season without trouble."

The sharp rap of a cane on the polished floor drew their attention. Lady Beatrice, Alexander's formidable grandmother, approached with an air of authority that commanded respect. Her eyes, sharp and discerning, missed nothing.

"Alexander, Nathaniel." Lady Beatrice greeted them with an imperious nod. "I trust you are both enjoying the ball?"

"Indeed, Grandmother." Alexander bowed slightly. "It is a splendid evening."

Nate bowed much lower and kissed the back of Lady Beatrice's proffered hand.

The older woman's gaze shifted to where Mary was still conversing with Sebastian. Her eyes narrowed, and she turned back to Alexander with a steely expression. "Why do you permit that scoundrel Blackwood to converse with our sweet Mary?"

Alexander glanced at Nate before replying. "Satterfield introduced him. I could hardly whisk her away without attracting the attention we are trying to avoid. We are keeping a close watch, Grandmother. Nate and I both share your concerns about Blackwood."

"Satterfield is only a little better. It is a great pity he became so close to the family." Lady Beatrice's lips pursed in disapproval. "Blackwood is a menace. His reputation is abysmal, and I will not have him tarnishing the Darrow family's name further."

Nathaniel stepped forward. "Lady Beatrice, I will ensure Mary's safety. She deserves better than Blackwood's attentions, and I intend to see that she receives it."

Lady Beatrice's stern expression softened slightly as she regarded him. "I trust you, Nathaniel. You have integrity. Just see that Mary's good name remains unscathed by this evening's events."

Nate nodded, his resolve strengthening. "You have my word, Lady Beatrice."

With a last nod, she moved on, her presence leaving a wake of whispered admiration and respect among the guests.

"Thank you, Nate." Alexander clasped his shoulder. "She may be formidable, but she only wants what is best for Mary."

Nate smiled slightly. "As do I."

As the end of the evening approached, Blackwood headed in Mary's direction again. Nate almost collided with one of the waiters in his haste to be rid of his champagne.

He'd be damned if he would let that cad hog the last waltz of the evening. He made his way across the ballroom, intent on claiming her for both the graceful and romantic waltz that was about to start and the lively Sir Roger de Coverley that would conclude the dance set. Mary was momentarily alone, and he wasted no time in extending his hand.

"Lady Mary, may I have the honour of the final two dances?"

Mary looked up at him, and her face lifted in a bright smile. "My dance card is free, and yes, you may, Lord Everhart."

Chapter Three

Mary was almost ready to resign herself to leaving without seeing Lord Everhart again when she felt a presence behind her.

"Lady Mary, may I have the honour of the final two dances?"

The familiar voice made her heart skip a beat. She turned to find Nathaniel standing there, a warm smile on his face.

Mary's heart soared, and she gave him a bright smile as she accepted.

Nate led her onto the dance floor for the waltz and leaned closer. "Please, call me Nate. All my friends do."

He wanted to be friends. Mary gazed at him, her heart fluttering. "Very well, Nate. But only if you call me Mary."

"Mary, it is." His eyes twinkled with amusement.

They waltzed, and Mary felt as if she were floating. Nate wasn't as handsome as Sebastian. He was more attractive in a rugged, windswept way, and his charm and playfulness were irresistible. Their movements flowed together, their conversation jumping from one topic to another without missing a beat.

"Did you know that the royal fern is quite rare?" Nate asked.

"Of course." Mary lifted her brow. "But did you know it thrives best in moist, shady areas?"

Nate chuckled. "Perhaps we should start a botanical society, just the two of us. We could call it the Society of Fern Enthusiasts."

Mary laughed, feeling a sense of lightness and joy that she hadn't experienced all evening. "I would join in a heartbeat."

Nate grinned. "I can see it now... our meetings held in the most secretive of greenhouses, discussing the scandalous growth rates of various ferns."

"Scandalous, indeed!" Mary's laughter rang out. "I fear we might shock the ton with our botanical escapades."

"Let them recoil in shock." Nate grinned back. "I believe we should start with the infamous Maidenhair Fern. I've heard it's quite the troublemaker."

Mary shook her head, still smiling. "Oh, it is. And then perhaps we can move on to the rather elusive Ghost Fern."

"Perfect. Though, I must admit, my favourite is the ever-so-dignified Royal Fern. It's the genuine aristocrat of the plant world."

"Well, we must give it the respect it deserves."

Their banter continued throughout the dance, leaving Mary breathless with delight. Nate's genuine interest in her passion for botany made her feel seen and appreciated. There was no need for empty flattery. Their connection was based on mutual respect and shared interests.

As the final strains of the waltz faded, the musicians struck up the lively tune of the Sir Roger de Coverley. Nate grinned at Mary. "Shall we?"

Mary nodded, enjoying herself too much to hide her pleasure, and they joined the other couples for the high-spirited dance. The steps were fast and intricate, but Nate's steady presence by her side gave her confidence. She laughed and twirled, enjoying the freedom and pure exhilaration.

"Careful now," Nate teased as they moved through the lively figures. "We wouldn't want to be the first botanical society members to cause a scene at a ball."

"Speak for yourself," Mary shot back. "I think we'd make quite the impression."

As the dance continued, Mary found herself lost in the moment.

Nate's easy humour and genuine charm made the time fly by. She couldn't remember the last time she had felt so at ease in her own skin. The music, the laughter, the shared smiles—all of it combined to create a memory she knew she would cherish.

The dance left her breathless but laughing. As the last notes played and the couples bowed to one another, Mary and Nate shared a lingering look. There was a depth in his gaze that hinted at a connection far beyond the surface.

Mary's interest in Nate solidified. She was determined to get to know him better, to explore the bond they had forged. As he escorted her back to Eleanor, she felt a flutter of delight in her chest.

"Thank you, Nate," she whispered, her eyes shining with gratitude. "This evening has been wonderful."

"The pleasure was all mine, Mary. I look forward to our next encounter."

With a final bow, he left her with Eleanor, who raised an eyebrow in amusement. "You seem quite taken with Lord Everhart. He is already Nate, I see."

Mary blushed but couldn't hide her smile. "He is...different. In a good way."

Eleanor smiled. "I'm glad to hear it. He's a good man, Mary. Just follow your heart."

As the evening ended, Mary felt a sense of hope and excitement for the future. She had stepped into society, faced the challenges of her first ball, and discovered a connection that promised something special. With Nate's warm presence lingering in her mind, she couldn't wait to see what the rest of the season would bring.

Chapter Four

Sunlight through half open curtains woke Mary the morning after the Carlisle's ball. Excitement from the evening still lingered, memories dancing through her mind. She smiled as she recalled the waltz with Nate and the lively banter they had shared.

Her maid, Emily, entered the room with a tray of tea and a bright smile. "Good morning, Lady Mary. Did you sleep well?"

Mary sat up, her smile widening. "I did, Emily. It was a wonderful evening."

"I heard you were the belle of the ball." Emily set the tray down and pulled back the curtains to let the sunshine flood in. "Shall we get you dressed for the day?"

"Yes, please." Mary slipped out of bed, grabbed a cup of welcome tea, and moved to the dressing table.

Emily helped her into a morning gown of pale pink and blue hydrangeas on delicate white muslin. "I expect you will have a fair number of admirers calling today. There's already a mountain of flowers and calling cards downstairs."

Mary laughed. "Is that so? Well, I suppose I shall have to see who they are from."

Emily tied the ribbon at the back of Mary's gown and picked up the hairbrush. "Do tell, my lady. Who was the most charming of them all?"

"Lord Blackwood was charming and is very attractive to look at, and several dance partners were rather fun. But Lord Everhart—Nate—he was so genuine and kind."

Emily's eyes twinkled with mischief. "Nate, is it? That sounds rather intimate."

Mary jutted out her chin. "He asked me to call him that. He's a dear friend of Eleanor and Alexander."

Emily laughed. "I remember you having quite the crush on him."

"I did not." A warm flush spread from Mary's cheeks to her ears.

Emily just lifted her brow and continued brushing Mary's hair.

So much for keeping her crush a secret. But Eleanor had warned her that a lady's maid learns all her lady's secrets. "Why do you think I had a crush?"

"Well, let me see." Emily tapped her chin as if deep in thought. "Do you remember sixteen-year-old Mary blushing bright red whenever Lord Everhart entered the room? You stole glances at him, hoping to catch his eye without being too obvious. I'm sure your heart fluttered whenever he was near, and you spent a lot of time daydreaming."

Mary shook her head. "Pure conjecture!"

"Do you remember Alice's seventeenth birthday party?" Emily pushed on, regardless of Mary's emphatic denial. "It was a sunny afternoon, and we had a small celebration, right here in the garden. It was my first few weeks in this role, and I was still following you around like a shadow. You stood next to Lord Everhart in the garden, smoothing your wrinkle-free dress and tucking a non-existent stray curl behind your ear. He said something like 'It's a beautiful day, isn't it, Mary?' You blushed crimson and prattled on about how you helped to plant the roses — which looked mighty fine, by the way. You were like a jingly puppy."

"Was not." Mary scowled at Emily in the mirror.

But she remembered the party well. She'd wanted to impress Nate with her knowledge and involvement in the garden, hoping he would notice her efforts. He'd said that she must have quite the green thumb, and her heart soared at the compliment. She tried to hide her excitement, but her hands fidgeted with her dress, betraying her nerves. Fiddlesticks! She'd forgotten that Emily was alongside her that day.

"Well, I'm glad to hear of his genuine and kind character. I've always liked him. A gentleman who doesn't put on airs is worth his weight in gold." Emily arranged Mary's hair into a simple yet elegant style. "And what about Lord Blackwood? I heard you danced with him. He's quite the charmer."

Mary hesitated, recalling her conversation with Eleanor. "I danced with him, just the once, of course. Lord Satterfield introduced him as his nephew, but Eleanor warned me about him. She said he has a reputation as a rake."

Emily nodded. "It's always wise to be cautious. But you've got a good head on your shoulders. Just trust your instincts."

Mary smiled, appreciating Emily's straightforward advice. "Thank you, Emily. I will."

As they finished preparing, Emily handed Mary a small vial of lavender water. "A little something to keep you refreshed throughout the day."

Mary dabbed a bit on her wrists and neck, the soothing scent calming her nerves. "You always know just what I need."

Emily grinned. "That's what I'm here for. Now, dazzle them all at brunch."

Mary descended the grand staircase, her spirits high. The familiar chatter of her family gathered in the breakfast room welcomed her. Eleanor and Alice already sat at the table and engaged in animated conversation. Lord Weston, Eleanor's husband, sat beside her, reading the London Gazette. What surprised Mary most was her mother, the Dowager Countess Darrow. Thank goodness, the impending birth of her first grandchild, Olivia's child, seemed to have rekindled her spirit after a long period of grief and seclusion.

"Good morning, everyone." Mary took her seat.

"Good morning, Mary." Her mother smiled. "I heard you were quite the sensation at the ball last night."

Mary blushed. "It was a wonderful evening, Mother. I danced with so many partners, I could not keep their names straight."

Eleanor laughed. "Indeed, you did. And you handled it all with such grace."

Alice leaned forward. "Tell us more, Mary. What was the highlight for you?"

"The highlight was dancing with Lord Everhart. He asked me to call him Nate." Mary's cheeked flushed with warmth. "He's so different, so genuine."

Lord Weston looked up from his paper with a raised eyebrow. "At least Everhart is a decent man."

Lady Darrow nodded. "I'm glad to hear it. It's important to find someone who values you for who you are, not just for your dowry."

"Mother!" Mary spluttered out.

Just then, Eleanor squealed and grabbed the society columns. "You have you name in print, Mary."

Lady Beatrice tutted. "Hardly a thing to celebrate."

"I'm sure it's full of praise." Her mother patted Mary's hand.

"What does it say, Ellie?" Mary gripped her mother's fingertips. "Please don't tell me they labelled me 'a young woman of expectation'. I couldn't bear it." She dropped her face into her hands.

Everyone at the table except Lady Beatrice laughed out loud, though Alice tried to disguise her chortle with a delicate cough and her hand across her mouth.

"Well, let's see." Eleanor scrunched her brow as if trying to read. She was deliberately taking her time, and Mary was about to throttle her.

"The article is titled, 'A Night to Remember: Lady Mary Darrow Shines at the Carlisle Ball.' So, it can't be too bad."

Alice clapped her hands, a display of unladylike emotion that earned a glower from Lady Beatrice. She sat up straighter and steadied her hands on her lap. "Please tell us more, Eleanor."

"May I read aloud from your newspaper, darling?" Eleanor laid her delicate hand on Alexander's arm.

He gave her a nod, and Eleanor started reading.

"Amongst the glittering assembly of the ton, one debutante made a striking impression: Lady Mary Darrow, the third daughter of the late Earl of Grantham. Entering the ballroom with an air of grace and poise, Lady

Mary was the very picture of elegance. She wore a stunning gown of pale blue silk, adorned with delicate lace and intricate embroidery, which complemented her fair complexion and highlighted her captivating blue eyes."

Lady Beatrice sniffed and blew her nose.

Eleanor gasped. "Listen to this."

"Lady Mary possesses not only beauty but also intelligence and wit, making her a well-rounded debutante. What sets Lady Mary apart are the grace and poise with which she carries herself, making her one of the most sought-after debutantes of the season."

"One of the most sought-after." Alice clasped Mary's hand.

"Did you know 'grace and poise' means that you come with money?" Alice mock whispered to Mary.

"Girls." One word from Lady Beatrice was enough to quiet them both. She would no doubt lecture them later about the vulgarity of even mentioning money.

Eleanor drummed her fingertips on the table to get everyone's attention. "It lists the distinguished gentlemen you danced with and ends with..."

"The Times will continue to follow Lady Mary's season with keen interest, anticipating further delightful encounters and, perhaps the announcement of a most advantageous match."

Alexander took back the pages of his paper. "You must watch your step, Mary. No one loves a misstep more than the ton."

Hawkins, the butler, entered the room, his arms laden with bouquets of flowers. "Excuse the interruption, Lady Weston, but we've received many deliveries for Lady Mary and Lady Alice this morning. Where would you like me to have the vases set up?"

Eleanor answered, "In the drawing room and foyer, I think would be best, Hawkins."

Mary's eyes widened in surprise as Hawkins backed out of the room. Even the quickest glance at the bouquets in his arms revealed splendid blooms that filled the air with a heady mixture of fragrances.

"My goodness, Mary!" Alice exclaimed. "You really made quite the impression."

"I'm sure the bouquets are for both of us."

"Leave the cards attached, Hawkins." Eleanor winked at Mary. "I'm sure the ladies will want to read them all."

Mary hurried through her breakfast and with Alice in tow, darted into the drawing room.

"I doubt there are many for me." Alice trailed behind Mary.

"Don't be a goose. You were not a wallflower yourself." Mary pointed at Alice. "And don't mention my dowry. Mother already reminded me of how gentlemen are lining up for money rather than me."

"Now, who is being a goose? I'm sure most don't even know yet. Uncle Alex has kept it quiet."

Mary harrumphed. But she had to concede that Alexander had made the arrangements quietly for both herself and Caroline. No doubt for Alice too, though her dowry was smaller, as she had six sisters that Lady Beatrice was also sponsoring.

Not being one for airs and graces, Mary rolled up her sleeves and started helping the two maids, who were arranging the flowers into their best vases. She sorted through the cards attached to each bouquet, recognising names of acquaintances and new admirers. Amidst the many arrangements, one stood out—a magnificent bouquet brimming with colourful blooms.

"This one is from Lord Everhart, or Nate as he is to you." Alice wriggled her brows at Mary.

Mary gestured impatiently with her hands. "Hand it over."

Alice giggled as she moved onto a fresh bouquet and exclaimed that she had found four for herself.

Mary checked the note and saw that they were indeed for herself from Nate. There were deep red roses, symbolizing passionate love; white lilies, representing purity and virtue; and forget-me-nots, conveying a message of true love and remembrance. Interspersed among these were sprigs of rosemary for remembrance, ivy for fidelity, and lavender for devotion.

The card attached made her heart skip a beat. After telling her he couldn't call that day because of a business matter, she saw it was not just a simple note, but a poetic message in elegant script.

Lady Mary,
In your presence, roses pale,
Your beauty makes the stars grow frail.
Lilies pure, like your soul,
With you, I find myself whole.
Forget-me-nots, for I do not,
Your laughter, in my heart, is caught.
Till tomorrow brings us close,
Yours in spirit, Nate

Mary couldn't help but smile as she read the poetry sweet enough to warm her heart, yet polite enough to avoid the wrath of both Alexander and Lady Beatrice. The thoughtfulness of Nate's gesture, choosing flowers with meanings that spoke of admiration and sincerity, touched her core.

She placed the bouquet in a prominent spot, the verses lingering in her mind, each word a tender echo of the connection they had forged.

Eleanor interrupted her reverie. "I expect callers will besiege us today. You best get yourselves ready."

Mary clutched Nate's poem to her chest. "I only want to see one person, but he says he's busy today."

"I'm sure he will call on you as soon as he can, and you still must be polite and greet your other admirers with aplomb."

"Easy for you to say."

Eleanor laughed. "Yes, it is, but I remember my own nerves in my season."

Mary also remembered. Things had been so different before their papa died. "It feels such a long time ago."

"A lot has happened since then." Eleanor gave her a quick hug and a nudge toward the door. "Go on, Emily is waiting for you. I asked her to lay out your new duck egg-blue visiting dress."

Still clutching the note from Nate, Mary climbed the stairs to her bedroom.

Just before eleven, she stood in her dressing room, allowing Emily to adjust the lace trim on her morning gown. The soft, pastel blue fabric complemented her fair complexion. The high-waisted bodice and the matching short, fitted Spencer jacket accentuated her graceful figure. Her hair, styled in soft curls, was held back with a simple yet elegant ribbon.

"You look lovely, Lady Mary. Any visitor who is not enchanted must be blind."

Mary laughed as she smoothed the delicate folds of her skirt and adjusted the fichu around her neckline. "Thank you, Emily. Eleanor says I must greet any visitors with aplomb."

"I've no doubt you will, Miss." Emily handed Mary a pair of light lace gloves and a small, embroidered handkerchief.

Still smiling at the thought of Nate's gorgeous blooms and sweet poetry, Mary tucked his note into her jewellery box and made her way to the drawing room.

She settled into her favourite chair next to the fire, sunlight filtering through the lace curtains. The room was arranged to receive visitors, with a tea set ready on the small table beside Eleanor. Chattering lightly, Alice and Lady Beatrice followed her into the room. Alice sat on the chair next to Mary, while Lady Beatrice sat on the sofa next to Eleanor. Two armchairs were ominously positioned opposite Mary and Alice.

Mary glanced at the armchairs, a nervous flutter stirring in her stomach. She couldn't shake the feeling that they were about to conduct interviews rather than receive visitors.

She forced a light laugh. "I feel like we are about to interview applicants for the position of the most charming suitor."

"Tea, dearest." Eleanor poured for Mary and handed her a cup of steaming, fragrant brew. "It will help to settle your nerves."

Mary accepted the drink gratefully. "Where are Mama and Caroline?"

"Mama is keeping Caroline busy. We agreed six women in the drawing room could feel a little threatening for some of our callers."

Alice smoothed her skirts with trembling fingers. "We have received so many bouquets this morning. I can't help but wonder who will call."

The drawing room now resembled a lush garden, filled with the heady scents of roses, lilies, and lavender. Mary's gaze drifted to the flowers from Nate. How would it feel if he walked through the door, his warm smile lighting up the room? She hoped desperately that he would find time to visit despite his business matters.

"You made quite the impact last night." Lady Beatrice accepted a cup of tea. "It looks like a botanical garden in here. I wouldn't be surprised if we get more visitors than the local conservatory."

Mary blushed. "I didn't mean to. I just hope they don't expect me to waltz through the drawing room. I'm not sure I can manage that without tripping over my own feet."

"Avoid the rug." Alice poked her side. "We don't need you twirling into the fireplace."

Lady Beatrice lifted her brow in what looked like disapproval of their chatter. "I'm sure you two could charm your way out of any social catastrophe."

Hawkins entered and announced, "Lord Blackwood for Lady Mary."

Lady Beatrice set her mouth in a grimace. "He certainly has wasted no time."

Mary's heart gave a little flutter. "Should I say I'm not home?"

"He is well aware we are all home the day after the Carlisle's ball. It would be extremely rude to refuse his visit, Grandmother." Even though Hawkins had shut the door behind him, Eleanor whispered across the room.

Lady Beatrice fluttered her hand as if to say, *be it on your head.*

"Please show him in, Hawkins." Eleanor gifted Mary one of her confidence-boosting grins.

A moment later, Lord Blackwood entered the drawing room, his presence as magnetic as ever. He bowed deeply, a charming smile on his lips. "Good morning, ladies. What a rare pleasure to visit with four such beauties."

"Good morning, Lord Blackwood." Mary offered her hand. "Please, do have a seat."

Sebastian kissed the back of her hand, his intense gaze never leaving her face. He settled into the chair opposite her. Thankfully, the conversation flowed easily as they exchanged pleasantries about the previous evening's ball and the beautiful weather. The butler discreetly served tea, and Mary offered Sebastian a delicate porcelain cup.

"Thank you, Lady Mary." Sebastian accepted the tea with a nod, then glanced at Eleanor. "I must say, your home is as charming as its inhabitants."

Eleanor smiled warmly. "You are very kind, Lord Blackwood. We are delighted to have you visit this morning."

Lady Alice added with a twinkle in her eye. "Indeed, it is always a pleasure to have such agreeable company."

Lady Beatrice, with her usual authoritative presence and somewhat of a glare, gave a slight nod. "I trust you enjoyed the ball last evening?"

"Very much so, Lady Beatrice," Sebastian replied smoothly. "It was a splendid event, made all the more enjoyable by the delightful company."

Sebastian reached into his coat pocket and produced two small, elegantly wrapped packages. "Lady Mary, Lady Alice, I brought you both a little something as a token of my admiration."

Mary and Alice exchanged surprised glances before unwrapping the packages. Inside, they found delicate fans, intricately painted with scenes of gardens in full bloom. The craftsmanship was exquisite.

"They are beautiful, Lord Blackwood." Mary's eyes shone with appreciation. He had even been kind enough to get them both gifts. "Thank you so much."

"Indeed, they are lovely." Alice grinned, her delight obvious. "Such a thoughtful gift."

"I am pleased you like them." Sebastian's smile widened. "You mentioned your fondness for gardens in our conversation, and I thought these might be fitting tokens."

Polite to a fault, after about fifteen minutes of the expected small talk, Sebastian gracefully rose to take his leave.

Before departing, he turned to Eleanor. "Lady Weston, would you and your family do me the honour of accompanying me to the theatre in a few days' time? The School for Scandal is playing at the Theatre Royal, Drury Lane, and I would be delighted if you would join me."

Mary's eyes lit up with excitement, but she held her tongue in case Lady Beatrice sent him away with a flea in his ear.

Eleanor exchanged a quick glance with Lady Beatrice before

answering. "That sounds wonderful, Lord Blackwood. We would be delighted."

Mary allowed her smile to broaden. "Thank you for the invitation, Lord Blackwood. We all look forward to it."

"Yes, it will be a delightful outing," Alice added.

A sense of satisfaction filled her as Hawkins showed Sebastian out. The morning call had been brief but pleasant, a perfect start to the day and a promising continuation of their acquaintance. Eleanor and Lady Beatrice exchanged another knowing glance, each quietly assessing the interaction with interest.

"Papa took me last year. The School for Scandal is such a witty play," Alice said. "I can't wait to see it again."

"I've heard so much about it, but this will be my first time seeing it." Mary sucked in a breath. "Do you think he meant the invitation for the whole family? I'm sure Mama and Caroline would enjoy it, and Alexander also, of course."

Eleanor laughed. "I can't imagine Alexander letting us go without a male escort."

"I expect the box seats eight and is spacious enough to add an extra chair if necessary. I'll send a note to Blackwood and inform him that there will be seven of us attending." No one argued with Lady Beatrice as she left the room.

Mary's thoughts drifted to Sebastian. His company had been delightful, and she found herself looking forward to the theatre outing with genuine anticipation. He had shown her nothing but kindness and respect, and she couldn't reconcile the charming man she had accompanied with the rumours of his rakish behaviour.

Despite her growing affection for Nate, Sebastian's charm was difficult to resist.

<h1 style="text-align:center">Chapter Five</h1>

Nate took a deep breath as he stood outside Alexander's grand townhouse. The rich scent of polished wood and the distant hum of London at midday filled the air.

He had spent too much time yesterday replaying the events of the Carlisle ball in his mind rather than focusing on his business meetings. His lordship couldn't stop thinking about Mary. The memory of their waltz, the way her laughter bubbled up like a melody, and the sparkle in her eyes that rivalled the chandelier above them had kept him awake to the early morning.

He was ready to admit that the lovely and spirited young woman had captured more than just his interest.

Now, as he prepared to speak with Alexander, her brother-in-law and guardian, his heart pounded. Though whether it was anticipating seeing Mary again or nerves at talking to Alexander, it was difficult to say.

Hawkins led him through the house, the soft carpet muffling their steps. They reached Alexander's study, and Nate walked into the comforting scent of leather-bound books and the crackle of a fire in the hearth.

Alexander looked up from his large mahogany desk, papers and writing pads strewn about, and grinned. "Nate, old chap. What brings you here? Couldn't you wait to lose another game of chess?"

Nate chuckled, some of his tension easing at Alexander's teasing. "Not quite. I want to speak with you about Mary."

Alexander's grin widened, and he leaned back in his chair, crossing his arms over his chest. His tone was teasing. "Ah, I thought as much. You've taken quite a shine to my sister-in-law, haven't you?"

A flush of heat crept up his neck. "That is the truth, Alexander. I won't deny it, but I don't want to overstep or make her uncomfortable so early in the season. I want to make sure you find my attentions toward her acceptable."

Alexander studied him for a moment.

For several horrible seconds, Nathaniel realised he had no alternative plan if Alexander told him to back off. But before he could cycle into a pit of worry, Alexander nodded, his expression softening.

"I appreciate you asking my opinion, and I'm pleased that you and Mary have hit it off so well. She's taken a liking to you, and I know I can trust you to treat her with the respect she deserves."

Relief washed over Nate, but before he could respond, Alexander continued, "There's something you should know. Blackwood has invited Mary, all of us, I believe, to the theatre the day after tomorrow. He's been rather insistent, and it's clear he's taken an interest in her.

A sharp pang of jealousy hit Nate at the mention of Blackwood. The man had been far too attentive to Mary at the ball, and it had left him unsettled.

"Blackwood can't have serious intentions. He's never shown much interest in any lady except for those he can bed without rancour."

Alexander's expression darkened. "Mary is lovely, but I'm sure his interest is more in her dowry than in Mary herself. I've heard whispers about his financial troubles."

Nate's worry deepened, and he leaned forward in his chair. "Her dowry? I've heard nothing about—"

"I settled thirty thousand pounds on her and her younger sister to help their marriage prospects, and I thought it had arranged it all with stealth. Eleanor was worried that with all the scandal attached to the Darrow name, they'd be ignored in the marriage mart."

Nate whistled. "Fifteen thousand each. That will attract a lot of young men looking for a wealthy bride."

"Thirty thousand each. I was feeling absurdly generous that day."

"Good Lord." Nate straightened. "Damnation. That is a princely sum. She will have every lordling in the land vying for her hand."

"She did." Alexander strode to the drinks cabinet and poured two large brandies. "I'm sure her dance card could have filled three times over."

"How the hell did Blackwood find out?" Nate's jaw was stiff with annoyance, but he was also curious.

"Heavens only knows. But it's not the first time he's come into sensitive information well before the ton grabs hold of it."

"He must use a network of spies."

"Would make sense how he can always find the bored married women looking for affection, and the widows ready to leave their grief behind."

Nate stiffened his spine. "I hope you don't think that I..." He couldn't continue, surely not. His friend wouldn't think him to be such a cad as to chase Mary for her dowry. Would he?

Alexander handed over a brandy and lifted his glass in a toast. "You, my friend, are one of the most honest men I know. Plus, I know how much you earn from your legal work and your outrageously successful investments."

Nate nodded, though without enthusiasm. His investments were doing well. So much so, he'd recommended several to Alexander.

Nathaniel took a large swallow of the brandy and enjoyed the burn down his throat. "I've seen firsthand how Blackwood operates. He leaves a trail of broken hearts in his wake. The way he looked at Mary last night —it was predatory. Regardless of how Mary feels towards me, I will not stand by and let her be his next victim."

Alexander nodded, his eyes meeting Nate's with a steady gaze. "I'll ensure that Mary and the other ladies are never alone with Sebastian, including at the theatre. If he behaves as anything less than a complete gentleman, I will see him off myself."

"If he behaves like anything less than a gentleman, his face will meet my fist."

Alexander's grin returned, and he clapped Nate on the shoulder. "It's rare to see you riled up, my friend."

He huffed, somewhere halfway between annoyance and embarrassment. "Mary is worth getting riled over."

"On that, we agree." Alexander lifted the carafe. "Do you need another brandy before we join the ladies?"

Nate had almost forgotten his second reason for calling at the Weston's townhouse that afternoon. Another brandy was a necessity. As they sipped their drinks in companionable silence, he'd decided to attend the play. His brother's box was opposite Blackwood's. Thankfully, theatre lighting was designed for the audience to see both the stage and one another. Being seen was, after all, as important as watching the play. With opera glasses, he could make out some of what happened in Blackwood's box.

When the two men joined the ladies in the drawing room. Mary looked up as they entered, her expression lighting up when she saw Nate. His heart skipped a beat at the sight of her, and he crossed the room to stand beside her.

"I trust you are well, Lady Mary." He pressed a gentle kiss to her hand.

"Very well, and I thank you for the wonderful bouquet." She stood and gestured to the blooms, then clasped his arm and lowered her voice. "And for the wonderful verse. I was more touched than you could imagine.

"I'm glad. The blooms were easy to organise, but the verse took me a little while to perfect." Just a little lie. The verse had taken him almost the entire time between getting home from the ball and getting up to breakfast.

It was gratifying to see the pleasure on Mary's face, and his bouquet in prime position on the pedestal by the window, the natural light enhancing the beauty of the flowers.

"Will you be attending Lady Pembroke's garden party tomorrow afternoon?"

Mary's face brightened, and she nodded with enthusiasm. "We were discussing whether to attend this morning. Alice and Lady Beatrice didn't seem to think that many marriageable men would bother going. Though I've heard her garden is a sight to behold, and I'd love to see it."

"Alice and Lady Beatrice may well have a good point, but Lady Pembroke's garden is picturesque. Humphrey Repton designed it, and it is a brilliant example of how he integrates gardens with the surrounding landscape, creating the most pleasing and harmonious effect."

Mary gasped. "Humphrey Repton. The leading figure in English garden design? I have devoured all his 'Red books'. The before and after sketches are so inspiring."

Nate lowered his voice. "She also has a magnificent conservatory, full of rare and interesting ferns."

"Oh, Nate. I must go." She squeezed his arm.

"I will be delighted to take you if Alexander can't attend."

"I'm sure my maid can attend us as chaperone if no one—"

"A single maid isn't sufficient chaperone, my dear." Lady Beatrice rapped her cane on the floor.

They had been so captivated by each other's gazes that neither heard her approaching despite the tap-tap of her cane on the floor.

Lady Beatrice gave them a nod. "Eleanor and I will accompany you."

"Accompany them where, Grandmother?" Eleanor swivelled to face the trio.

"Lady Pembroke's garden party tomorrow afternoon."

"Oh, yes indeed. Lady Pembroke is a hoot."

With that matter settled to everyone's satisfaction, attention drifted away from Nate and Mary. Still standing close together in the room's corner, they chatted together for some time, the conversation flowing. Nate found himself captivated by her wit and charm, and the time slipped by unnoticed until the clock chimed, reminding him it was time to take his leave.

Mary walked him to the door, her arm linked with his. "Thank you for calling on us, Nate. I look forward to seeing you tomorrow.

He squeezed her hand. "I will collect you and whoever is travelling with us at two forty. Until then, Mary."

She smiled at him so sweetly, his heart swelled with affection.

As he stepped out into the cool evening air, a renewed sense of determination filled Nate. The crisp breeze carried the distant sounds of the city getting ready for the evening entertainments, a stark contrast to the light and warmth of the drawing room. A sobering contrast to Mary's sweetness.

Alexander was right. He rarely behaved with anger, but Mary was worth getting riled over.

The young woman he was thinking of as his was worth protecting.

Chapter Six

Mary was dressed and ready long before the allocated time for Nate to collect them in his carriage. Alexander had declared he could not stomach a garden party at Lady Pembroke's, that, or any other afternoon. Mother and Caroline were again in attendance upon Olivia, who was "as fat as a plump partridge and as grumpy as a wet hen" according to Caroline. Mary couldn't wait to be an aunt, and that day couldn't come soon enough.

Despite knowing that a lady should never show too much enthusiasm, she sat in the drawing room with the curtain pulled back, so she had a clear view of the street. The sun shone as Nate's polished landau pulled up in front of the townhouse, wheels gleaming. The folding roof was open, so a wonderful gentle breeze and warm sunlight would spill into the carriage. A thrill of excitement coursed through Mary's body. It was going to be such a splendid day.

Two footmen followed their small group outside and assisted Eleanor, Alice, and Lady Beatrice into the landau.

Lady Beatrice, with a twinkle in her eye, directed the seating arrangements. "Eleanor, Alice, Mary, sit together on the other side. Nathaniel, you shall sit here, next to me."

Nate met Mary's gaze and winked. She couldn't suppress a smile.

Lady Beatrice's mischievous manoeuvre had seemed to meet every requirement of a chaperoned outing, but had in fact seated Nate opposite her, and now they nestled against the carriage door. Given Nate's height, and that she was the tallest of the sisters, their knees almost touched.

She could have moved back in the seat and stiffened her spine, but what was the fun in that?

Nate's leg brushed against hers, and a shiver of anticipation travelled up her spine. He adjusted his position, and his knee pressed gently against hers. Her breath caught, and she dared to glance at him.

He pretended to gaze out the window, but he was watching her, a spark of playful intent dancing in his eyes.

Beneath the concealing folds of her skirt, Nate's foot nudged hers. She bit her lip to keep from laughing. A sense of daring she had never felt before rose within her. Face showing nothing, Mary hoped, she nudged him back.

Every subtle shift of their feet sent a thrill coursing through her veins. Alice and Eleanor argued with Lady Beatrice about something or another, and the clandestine interaction went unnoticed. Nate hid laughter behind a few snorts, and she revelled in their shared delight at this hidden exchange. His smile broadened into a conspiratorial grin, and her pulse quickened with anticipation.

The roads seemed busier than ever, and the vehicle stopped repeatedly. Every bump and jostle bounced them closer, the touch of their knees more frequent. Mary felt a giddy sense of connection with Nate, one that transcended mere words.

The carriage set off again, and Alice nudged her. "Mary, tell us more about that rare orchid you are studying and sketching."

Mary blushed at the most unsubtle push to get her talking. She cleared her throat, trying to compose herself despite the thrilling proximity to Nate. "Well, you see, it's called the Ghost Orchid. It's quite an elusive little devil in the plant world."

Nate leaned forward, his eyes twinkling. "A ghost, you say. Should we be frightened?"

"Yes!" Mary played along, her voice dropping to a mock-whisper. "It haunts swamps in Florida and gives visitors, including botanists, the vapours."

Lady Beatrice chuckled. "My dear, I believe you're pulling our legs."

"Not at all, Lady Beatrice." Mary warmed to her subject. "This orchid is so pale and ethereal, it looks like it's floating in mid-air. No leaves to speak of, just roots clinging to trees like some botanical acrobat."

Alice piped up, "How unladylike! A plant without proper attire?"

Mary nodded. "It's quite the scandal in horticultural circles. And its bloom? It's more fleeting than a debutante's first season. Blink, and you'll miss it."

Nate's knee pressed against hers again as he leaned closer. "And how does one capture such a ghostly beauty?"

Mary's eyes sparkled with mischief. "With great difficulty, I'm afraid. It requires the attentions of a very rare giant Sphinx moth—"

Eleanor gasped in mock horror, while Alice dissolved into giggles.

"That's quite enough, young lady." Lady Beatrice fanned herself. "I believe this Ghost Orchid would be quite at home in Lady Pembroke's garden of curiosities."

She wasn't at all surprised at Lady Beatrice cutting her discourse short. Young ladies were not supposed to know about or understand plant pollination. But Mary had joined the Horticultural Society of London over a year ago, and while only men could enjoy formal membership, women could participate in botanical activities and horticultural pursuits. She'd met Miss Delaney there, as well as other talented illustrators, and aspired to be as skilled as they in her own sketching.

As the carriage jolted over a bump, Mary inched closer to Nate. She lowered her voice, speaking for his ears only. "You know, they say the Ghost Orchid is impossible to cultivate outside its natural habitat."

Nate's gaze locked with hers, his voice also low. "Some might say the same about certain feelings within the business-focused ton, Lady Mary. Yet here we are, nurturing something quite rare, indeed."

Mary's cheeks heated, and not just from the warmth of the day. She cast up a quick and silent prayer that this blossoming connection with Nate wouldn't prove as elusive as the Ghost Orchid itself.

Light-hearted banter and easy conversation filled the rest of the ride, the kind that felt natural and unforced. She couldn't remember the last time she had enjoyed such an outing.

When they arrived at Lady Pembroke's garden party, an enchanting sight greeted them. The gardens were a riot of colour, with blooming flowers and lush greenery stretching as far as the eye could see. Guests strolled along well tended paths, their laughter mingling with gentle harp music and birdsong.

With Lady Beatrice and Eleanor's blessing, Mary and Nate strolled arm in arm just ahead of their small group. After a short distance, Lady Beatrice detoured to talk with some of her oldest friends. Friends hailed Eleanor and Alice just a few steps further along.

Left alone, Mary and Nate continued along the path until they stumbled into a secluded nook surrounded by fragrant roses and tall hedges. It was a private paradise. A thrill of naughtiness filled Mary at being so hidden away with Nate. If Lady Beatrice saw her, there would be hell to pay!

"It's so peaceful here." Mary inhaled the sweet scent of the flowers. "So beautiful."

Nate nudged her to a small stone bench, so small they had to sit quite close together. Mary swallowed a hard lump in a thickening throat, now she had to contend with the warmth of Nate's thigh right next to her on the bench. His gaze softened as he looked at her. "I could spend all day in a place like this."

Mary had to break the spell that was wrapping her in knots.

"You see that climbing rose there?" She pointed to a vibrant pink bloom cascading over a nearby trellis. "When I was twelve, I cultivated the perfect rose. I spent an entire summer experimenting with different soils and pruning techniques. One day, I was so engrossed in my work, I didn't notice a bee landing on my arm. When I saw it, I jumped in fright and fell right into a thorny bush like that one!" She laughed, touching a series of small scars on her forearm. "I still have the marks to prove it."

Nate chuckled. "Your dedication is admirable, even if it came at a price. I have a similar tale from my travels in India." He gestured to a patch of vibrant marigolds nearby. "These remind me of the fields I saw there. One afternoon, I was sketching some stunning specimens when I heard a commotion. I looked up to find a mischievous monkey had stolen my hat and was using it as a flower basket."

"Oh, my!" Mary giggled, picturing the scene. What did you do?"

Nate grinned and leaned in even closer. "I ended up trading my pocket watch for my hat. The petty thief seemed quite pleased with the exchange, and I got some lovely marigolds as a bonus."

Their laughter mingled in the air, sweet as the perfume of the surrounding flowers. As their mirth subsided, Mary gazed into Nate's eyes, struck by how the dappled sunlight filtering through the leaves brought out flecks of gold in his irises.

"You know," Nate murmured, his hand inching closer to hers on the bench. "I've seen many wonders in my travels, but all pale compared to the beauty I find right here."

Mary's heart fluttered, knowing he meant more than just the garden. In this secluded paradise, surrounded by nature's splendour, she and Nate could have been the only two people in the world.

As they talked, Mary saw Nate in a new light. His charm gave way to reveal genuine kindness and depth. His thoughtful words and warm smile touched her in unexpected ways, stirring something deep within her. She was hyper-aware of his presence. The timbre of his voice sent pleasant shivers down her spine. She noticed the way his eyes crinkled when he laughed, the gentle strength in his hands as he gestured. Her heart quickened whenever their gazes met, and a warm flush crept up her neck.

At one point, their gazes locked and lingered. An unspoken connection sparked between them, charged with possibility. Dizzy with anticipation, Mary's breath caught in her throat, her lips tingling as if they already knew what was coming.

Nate leaned in slowly, giving Mary a moment to choose. She had no intention of pulling back, instead lifting her face so her bonnet wouldn't get in the way. Time seemed to stretch, her pulse loud in her ears. The warmth radiating from Nate's body penetrated her wherever they touched. Their lips met in a tender kiss.

A jolt of electricity shot through Mary. Her eyes fluttered closed as she lost herself in the sensation. Nate's lips were soft, his touch against her arms reverent. She breathed in his scent—a hint of cologne mixed with something male and uniquely him. The world around them faded away, leaving only this perfect moment.

Nate pulled back, and a pang of loss filled Mary. Her lips still tingled, and she had to resist the urge to touch them. She felt light and giddy, and a warm, bubbly feeling spread through her chest.

Nate's expression was soft, a question in his eyes. "Mary, I…"

"Don't apologise." She touched his hand, her skin buzzing where it met his. "That was nice."

Relief and happiness washed over his features, and they sat together in comfortable silence.

But Mary's inner world was alive with sensation. Nice? What an understatement. Her heart raced, her skin felt electrified, and a pleasant warmth spread through her body. The moment felt both monumental and simple, the start of something beautiful.

Suddenly, Alice stumbled into their secluded spot, their private reverie abruptly disturbed.

She lurched to the far corner and, on her hands and knees, retching up the contents of her stomach.

Nate pressed his handkerchief into Mary's hand and mumbled something about getting help and bringing his carriage around.

Mary's concern flared. Alice laboured her breathing, a sheen forming on her pale skin, her forehead feverish.

"Alice! What's wrong?" Mary rushed to her cousin's side.

"Don't know." Alice groaned. "One minute I was flirting and drinking punch, the next I was seeking a place to cast up my lunch. It hurts, Mary. Make it stop."

A tear squeezed from Alice's eye, and Mary pulled her close. "Never fear, dearest. I'll make you some ginger tea while we await the physician."

"Hate ginger tea," Alice mumbled.

"If you drink up your ginger tea, I'll let you have some of my peppermint lozenges."

Alice's only response was another long, low groan.

Nate returned with Eleanor in tow and a wet towel.

Eleanor took charge, questioning both Mary and Alice as she wiped Alice's face. "Can you walk to the carriage, my dear?"

"I don't know, hurts to stand." Alice sniffled.

"I'll carry her." Nate didn't wait for an answer. He plucked Alice from the ground. "Let's leave now, before anyone notices. I've already sent a boy for your family physician."

Mary collected Alice's elaborately embroidered reticule and a finely knit shawl she had dropped and followed behind.

"Try not to groan, dear. We'll pretend you had a fainting spell." Eleanor led the way to the front of the house. "One of her friends will return Lady Beatrice home so we will have a little more room in the carriage."

Eleanor jumped into the carriage and gestured to Nate. "I'll hold her on my lap. The carriage is almost wide enough for her to lie straight."

With great care, Mary and Nate helped Alice into the landau before slumping on the seat opposite. There were no footsies this time. They sat as far as they could from one another, and a tense silence marked the journey back, their earlier joy overshadowed by worry for Alice's health.

As they sped homeward, Mary glanced at Nate. She stretched her fingertips towards his on the leather between them. He did not move his gaze from the window, but slowly he reached out his own fingers and wrapped them around hers.

Eleanor narrowed her eyes at Mary but kept questions to herself. For now, at least. No doubt as soon as she saw Alice comfortably settled, Mary would face a grilling and possibly a lecture on appropriate behaviour with a man who was not yet more than a friend. Did anyone know about her quiet interlude with Nate?

What had she done? What if they were seen together in the secluded alcove? Such reckless behaviour was not like her at all.

Mary let out a sigh, her emotions a tumultuous mix of worry for Alice and lingering warmth from Nate's kiss. The carriage wheels clattered over cobblestones, each jolt a reminder of the precarious situation. She glanced at Nate, his brow furrowed. But was it with concern for Alice, or was he too replaying their stolen moment?

As they neared home, a fresh fear gripped her. What if someone witnessed their kiss and told Alexander? He would call out Nate, insist that he marry her. She liked Nate, liked him a lot. But that wasn't the way she wanted anyone to propose to her. Yet, even as anxiety twisted in her stomach, she couldn't bring herself to regret it. The memory of Nate's lips on hers sent a shiver through her that had nothing to do with the evening chill.

The carriage lurched to a stop. As they prepared to help Alice inside, Eleanor fixed Mary with a knowing look. *We'll talk later*, she mouthed.

Mary nodded, steeling herself for what was to come. Whatever happened next, she knew one thing for certain—her life would never be the same.

Chapter Seven

Mary smoothed the cool cloth over Alice's forehead, her cousin's eyes fluttering beneath closed lids. The physician's words echoed in her mind—too much sun, too much punch. Rest for forty-eight hours. She sighed, relieved it wasn't something more serious, yet guilt gnawed at her. Perhaps she would have noticed Alice's distress sooner if she hadn't been so wrapped up in Nate, if they hadn't broken away from the group.

A soft knock at the door pulled Mary from her thoughts. Eleanor stood in the doorway, her expression unreadable.

"Mary, dear, join me in my private sitting room. Alice will be fine for a few moments."

Mary's stomach clenched. She knew this moment was coming, but that didn't make it any easier. With a last glance at Alice, she rose and followed Eleanor down the hallway.

Eleanor's sitting room was a sanctuary of calm, all muted blues and creams. But as Mary perched on the edge of a delicate settee, she felt anything but calm. Eleanor poured tea from a silver pot, the clinking of porcelain filling the tense silence.

Eleanor settled into her favourite armchair. "Let's discuss what happened this afternoon."

Mary's fingers twisted in her lap. "Alice became ill—"

Eleanor cut in, "I saw you and Nate in the carriage, Mary. The way you reached for each other. Something happened between you two, didn't it?"

Heat rushed to Mary's cheeks. She opened her mouth, closed it again, then spoke, "After Lady Beatrice went to talk with friends, we... well... we sort of found a lovely private spot and we conversed."

"Just conversed?" Eleanor prodded.

Mary wriggled as if ants crawled over her skin. "We talked and we sat together. And, oh, Eleanor... we kissed."

Eleanor's eyebrows rose but she didn't seem shocked. "I see. And is this the first time you have kissed Nate or anyone else?"

"Yes! I would never dream of kissing random strangers," Mary exclaimed, then lowered her voice. "Yes. It was... unexpected. But not unwelcome."

Eleanor sipped her tea, studying Mary over the rim of her cup. "And what is happening between you and Nate? Are you courting?"

Mary's brow furrowed. "I'm not sure. We've been spending time together, talking. He makes me laugh. And when he kissed me..." she trailed off, lost in the memory.

"Mary." Eleanor's tone was gentle, but firm. "You must be careful. You know how quickly rumours can spread. If anyone observed you—"

"I know." Mary's earlier fears resurfaced. "I wasn't thinking. But, Eleanor, I care for him. I do."

Eleanor set down her teacup with a sigh. "I can see that. But you must consider your reputation, your future. Has Nate spoken of his intentions?"

Mary shook her head. "Not explicitly. But the way he looks at me, the things he says. I believe he cares for me too."

"Beliefs and feelings are fine, my dear, but in our world, we need more than that." Eleanor leaned forward, taking Mary's hand. "I'm not saying you should distance yourself from Nate. But you must be prudent. No more stolen kisses until his intentions are clear. Can you promise me that?"

Mary wanted to argue, to defend the purity of her feelings for Nate.

But she knew Eleanor was right. With a heavy heart, she nodded. "I promise."

Eleanor squeezed her hand. "Good girl. Now, why don't you tell me everything from the beginning? I want to understand what's blossoming between you two."

Excitement warred with trepidation as Mary recounted her interactions with Nate. The path ahead might be challenging, especially if someone had seen them kiss, but the memory of it gave her hope. Whatever came next, she was ready to face it.

The theatre was resplendent as always, its grand chandeliers casting a warm glow over the whispering audience. Mary adjusted her seat, her heart fluttering with excitement as she awaited the start of the play.

The theatre was one of her favourite escapes, a place where she could lose herself in the performance's magic. Mary inhaled, savouring the familiar scent of polished wood and velvet that permeated the grand building. The rising murmur of the crowd, the rustling of programs, all filled her with a sense of anticipation. This was her sanctuary, a place where reality faded, and dreams took centre stage.

Tonight, however, felt different. Alice was missing, still in her bed, resting. Eleanor sat between Alexander and Lady Beatrice, both distracted as Lady Beatrice complained of a stomachache.

Lord Blackwood settled in the empty seat beside her, and a note of discord crept into her reverie. His cologne, usually pleasant, seemed overpowering in the close confines of the theatre box. When his arm brushed hers, she tensed, unsure if it was accidental or deliberate.

She smoothed her hands across her lap and fidgeted with the lovely, beaded reticule that matched her lilac silk dress. It wasn't a colour she had worn before, but both Emily and Alice declared it perfect with her hair and eyes and swore it made her a picture of grace and charm.

She drew out the delightful fan Sebastian had gifted her and fanned her face.

Though the neckline was a modest bateau shape, and the puff

sleeves reached the top of her white kid gloves, she pulled the lace shawl over her shoulders. Something about Lord Blackwood's nearness sent shivers up her spine.

He leaned in close, his proximity filling her with unease. She dismissed her discomfort and tried to focus on the rising curtain and the opening scene. But as the play progressed, Sebastian's advances grew bolder.

He brushed his arm against hers again, and this time there was no doubt it was intentional. Mary found her attention divided between the stage and Lord Blackwood. His whispered comments, at first distracting, took on a more insistent tone.

Conscious that she was here as his guest, she shifted in her seat, her skin crawling with discomfort. She tried to create distance without causing offence, acutely aware of every inch between them.

"Please, Lord Blackwood, allow me to concentrate on the play." A tremor of anxiety ran through Mary's voice, but her jaw clenched with barely contained frustration. She cast a wary glance at her family, determined not to cause a scene. So she fixed a smile on her face before speaking again. "We can converse during the interval."

She hoped her gentle rebuke would suffice, but Lord Blackwood chuckled. His breath, warm against her ear, sent an involuntary shiver down her spine.

"Call me Sebastian, my sweet Mary." He moved his hand to rest on her arm, and her flesh prickled at his unwelcome touch.

Mary narrowed her eyes. Sweet, indeed. There was much more sarcasm than charm in that comment she'd wager. An icy dread settled in her chest as she realized her mistake. She should never have given him leave to use her first name at the ball.

"*Lord* Blackwood." She emphasised his title. "Sebastian. "I'm finding it difficult to follow the performance. Perhaps you might direct your attention to the stage."

Her plea, possibly the use of his first name, seemed to work. He pulled back. Mary felt a momentary rush of relief. Still too close for her liking, but they were no longer touching.

Her words seemed to amuse him, as did her reactions to his proximity. Indignation flickered in her chest. She was feeling like a mouse being toyed with by a smug cat. She would forever feel sorry for any poor creatures caught in a cat's claws.

It was almost time for the intermission when a deep groan came from Lady Beatrice. She gripped Eleanor's arm. "My dear, can you help me to the retiring room?"

As Eleanor struggled to help Lady Beatrice stand and walk, Alexander jumped up to help. He gripped his grandmother's elbow and turned to Mary. "Wait outside the box, please. I will return as soon as I can."

Mary stood, her heart leaping at the chance to escape. "I can help," she offered, desperate for any excuse to avoid being left alone with Lord Blackwood.

Alexander shook his head. "No need to make a scene, but we may need to leave during the intermission."

Mary strode from the dark theatre box, her legs trembling beneath her skirts, almost tripping in her haste to get away from Lord Blackwood. She stood in the brightly lit corridor, blinking against the sudden glare. A wave of vulnerability washed over her. It wasn't yet time for the intermission, and there were very few people about.

Blackwood exited the box and sauntered to her side. "So eager to drop my company, sweet Mary?" He stood too close again, his presence suffocating.

Mary took a deliberate step to the side and lifted her chin. "I find, sir, that one's eagerness for company is proportional to the quality of conversation offered."

Blackwood's eyebrows rose, but he chuckled again. "Such spirit! I enjoy a woman with fire in her veins."

Mary's eyes flashed. "And I, sir, enjoy a gentleman who can recognise when his attentions are unwelcome. Surely, a man of your standing can appreciate the value of discretion and decorum?"

Standing side on to the light, his angelic face took on shadows and angles, transforming his features into something almost sinister. "My dear Mary, you wound me. I thought we were enjoying a pleasant tête-à-tête."

"Pleasant for whom, I wonder?" Mary retorted, her voice low but sharp. "I had hoped, Lord Blackwood, that you might prove to be a man of sense and sensitivity. Pray, do not disappoint me further."

The cat-and-mouse game was wearing on her last nerve. Mary's pulse quickened, a primal instinct urging her to flee, but she refused to cower. She met his gaze, a steady challenge in her eyes that belied her outward composure.

As soon as Alexander was out of sight, Blackwood gripped her elbow hard. With surprising strength and speed, he pulled her towards his box, yanked the door open, and manoeuvred her inside towards the darkest corner before she could protest.

Trapped. Her world narrowed to the confined space of the theatre box trapping her with the cad. The door closed behind him, obstructing her view of the corridor and any hope of immediate rescue.

Too shocked to think straight, she still twisted out of his grip and spun to face him. "How dare you—"

He took a step toward her, slow and languorous, as if he had all the time in the world.

"Lord Blackwood, I insist you open this door at once." Mary's voice trembled a little despite her effort to sound firm.

Blackwood's eyes gleamed with malicious intent as he advanced on her. "Come now, sweet Mary. We're alone at last."

She pointed her fan at him as if it were a weapon. "If you call me Sweet Mary one more time, I'll—"

"You will what, my dove? Does that please you more?"

"I cannot think of any reason I will ever speak to you again, but if an occasion arises, you may call me Lady Mary."

He laughed so loudly that half the audience must have heard him. But no, the interval had started, and people were noisily rising from the seats.

He closed the distance between them and pulled her to him. The cad attempted to kiss her, but she twisted her head, his lips brushing her cheek instead of her mouth. Her heart raced, her mind whirling. How could she extricate herself without causing a scene from which her reputation would never recover? She was acutely aware of her family's presence not far away, and of the potential scandal if she reacted more like a harridan than a lady. Yet every instinct screamed at her to fight or flee.

She could scream, but the last thing she wanted was to draw attention to herself.

She stamped on his foot, but the delicate silk slippers she wore were unlikely to cause any harm. He just laughed and tightened his arm around her waist, his body pressed too close. His hot breath drifted over her neck, and revulsion coursed through her veins. Her mind raced, searching for a way out of this predicament.

Just as Mary prepared to scream, consequences be damned, a sharp knock came at the door.

"Mary? Are you in there?" Nate's voice, muffled but unmistakable, came through the wood.

Blackwood gave her a small push. She darted around him and threw open the door.

"Nate." She stumbled into his broad chest in her haste to exit the box.

Nate steadied her, his concerned gaze taking in her appearance, which was almost certainly dishevelled, before hardening as it landed on Blackwood. "Is everything alright here?"

Mary straightened, finding strength in his presence. "It is now. I was just leaving."

"Blackwood."

As Mary tried to re-pin the tendrils of hair that had escaped her coiffure, she marvelled Nate could infuse so much menace into just one word.

The bounder stepped out of the box, his gaze narrowing. "Come now, Everhart. You're not suggesting anything untoward?"

Nate's jaw clenched. "I'm suggesting nothing, Blackwood. I'm concerned for Lady Mary's well-being."

"How chivalrous," he sneered. "Tell me, do you always lurk about waiting to play the white knight?"

"Only when there are wolves about." Nate's voice, low and dangerous, sent a shiver of excitement through Mary.

Blackwood's eyes flashed with anger. "Mind your tongue, Everhart. You forget your place."

"And you forget yours," Nate shot back. "A true gentleman would never compromise a lady's reputation."

Blackwood glowered at them both, but with the other patrons now filling the corridor for the interval, he seemed to think better of causing a scene.

He brushed past them, his shoulder bumping into Nate's. "This isn't over, Everhart. Until next time, Lady Mary."

As Blackwood disappeared into the crowd, Mary shivered. Was that a threat?

Chapter Eight

Once Blackwood was out of earshot, Nate turned to Mary. The air itself was thick with tension, muffled sounds of the theatre crowd sounding distant and unreal.

She placed her hand on his arm, her fingertips trembling so much he covered them with his own. Even through their gloves, the warmth sent a jolt through his body and ignited a fierce protectiveness.

"You are safe now." Despite rising anger, he kept his tone low and reassuring.

Mary nodded, but her face was pale, almost ghostly. Damn the man to hell and back. Nate's jaw clenched involuntarily.

He softened his gaze as he tried to quell the rage bubbling inside him. "Are you truly alright, my love?" The endearment just slipped out.

Mary gave him a small smile, but it didn't reach her eyes. "I am, thanks to you. Your timing was impeccable."

"Did Blackwood hurt you?" The question came out harsher than he intended, his imagination conjuring up scenario's, each one worse than the last.

"I think he just wanted to kiss me." She swallowed, her throat working. But when she lifted her gaze to his, her eyes were clear, and chin held high. "I didn't let him though."

The corridor filled with theatre patrons, and Nate stepped back a little. Perfumes and colognes mingled in a dizzying cloud, the rustling of silk gowns and murmuring of voices seeming to press in on them.

He hadn't planned to attend the theatre that night until he learned Blackwood had invited Mary and her family. But thank God he had.

From his seat, he'd kept his opera glasses focused on Mary, observing her interactions with Blackwood. The cad sat too close, and it wasn't long before he noticed the discomfort etched on Mary's face. The sight made his blood boil. When the box emptied just before interval, he had almost stopped watching. But then he caught sight of movement at the rear of the box. The hair at the back of his neck had risen—something was wrong.

Nate had decided he couldn't stand by and watch any longer. He'd navigated swiftly through the theatre, moving from one side to the other as fast as his long legs could take him without breaking into a run. His heart pounded as he had reached Blackwood's seating box, and without hesitation, he rapped on the door, his knuckles still stinging from the force.

He'd rather they stung from punching Blackwood in the face, but that would have created a scene none of them wanted.

Speaking of family, where the hell were they?

"Surely, Alexander did not leave you here alone with him." Nate ground out the question, tasting bile and ready to land a fist on Alexander's face as soon as he saw him.

"He did."

"Damnation."

Mary flinched, perhaps at the anger in his tone. Guilt washed over him and tempered the anger circling in his gut.

"Forgive my language, Mary. I'm afraid Blackwood has made me furious. And I feel like wringing Alexander's neck."

She gently touched his arm. "It would have been alright if Lord Blackwood hadn't dragged me back into the box. The light is bright enough, and the intermission was only minutes away."

"Why leave you at all, my love?" The endearment slipped out again, and this time, Nate kept his gaze firmly on Mary's face.

"Lady Beatrice became very ill, unable to even stand unaided.

Eleanor tried, but Alexander had to help them to the retiring room. He wouldn't have imagined…"

Mary's voice trailed off.

Alexander wouldn't have thought for one moment that Blackwood would attack her in such a way, but the thought did little to settle the anger Nate was directing toward him.

Nate gripped her hand again, marvelling at the strength within delicate bones and soft skin. "Shall we find your family?"

"Alexander said to wait here."

Her usual spark was missing, which hit Nate like a physical blow. Damn it, he should call Blackwood out. But he couldn't without bringing attention to his attempt to ravish Mary, and that would destroy her reputation. He should marry her immediately, before Blackwood tried again, and he wasn't around to step in.

He turned his gaze back to Mary, to find her gazing back. She blushed the prettiest of pinks and quickly lowered her gaze. The sight of her heightened colour brought a rush of tenderness mixed with a fierce desire to protect her.

Now was not the best time or place. But how much time did they have before gossip started? If he'd noticed Mary's discomfort from the other side of the theatre, then who else had noticed? The thought of wagging tongues and ruined reputations stiffened his spine.

Nate's expression grew serious. "Mary, I've been meaning to speak with you about us. About the future." He paused, taking a deep breath, his heart hammering against his ribs.

"I'm sorry Mary—" Alexander startled them both, his voice cutting through the moment.

Nate's fists clenched. "Weston, you cad, you promised you would look after her."

Alexander paled. "What happened?"

"Not here, please. I'd like to go home." Mary blinked as if to ward off tears, her lashes glistening in the lamplight.

Alexander gave a curt nod. "I've already sent Grandmother and Eleanor back in the carriage."

"Then allow me to return you both home." Nate would rather have enjoyed leaving Alexander to find his own way back, but that would just delay the opportunity to find out his excuse and give him the thumping he deserved.

The trip back to Weston's townhouse passed in stilted silence. Mary obediently sat next to Alexander, her knees pressed together, and hands twisted in her lap. Nate longed to pull her to him, to offer comfort and protection, but the expression on Alexander's face had turned thunderous, the tension in the carriage palpable.

As soon as they arrived, he walked Mary inside before excusing himself and striding after Alexander to his study. Each step felt laden with purpose, his muscles coiled tight with anger and anticipation.

The door to the study closed with a soft click, sounding more like the sealing of a tomb than the door snicking shut behind him. Alexander's ridiculously large desk, the scent of leather and old books, his friend's room usually brought comfort. Not this evening. Now it only heightened his agitation.

Alexander leaned against his desk, his fingers trailing along the polished wood as if seeking an anchor. His gaze remained fixed on the floor. "Explain." His tight voice wavered with barely controlled emotion.

"You left her alone with Blackwood." Nate took a deep breath, willing himself to remain calm. "He tried to force himself on her."

Alexander's face drained of colour, his knuckles turning white as he gripped the edge of the desk. "I didn't think—"

"No, you didn't think," Nate cut in, his voice rising. "You left your sister-in-law, your responsibility, alone with a man well known for his less than honourable intentions."

The words hung in the air, heavy and accusatory. Alexander seemed to shrink under their weight, his shoulders slumping. When he finally spoke, his voice was barely above a whisper. "How bad was it?"

Nate ran a hand through his hair, frustration clear in every movement. "Bad enough. If I hadn't arrived when I did..." He let the sentence trail off, unable to voice any of the terrible scenarios that were running through his mind on repeat.

Alexander sank onto the leather ottoman, his face a mask of guilt and horror. "God, what have I done?"

For a moment, Nate felt a flicker of pity for his friend. But then the image of Mary's pale, frightened face flashed through his mind, and his anger surged.

"You've put Mary in an impossible position. If word gets out, her reputation will be ruined. And it's not just her—your entire family could be affected."

Alexander looked up, his eyes meeting Nate's for the first time since they entered the study. "What can we do?"

Nate paced the room, his footsteps muffled by the thick carpet. "We need to act. We must deal with Blackwood, but discreetly. And Mary..." He paused, his heart racing as he contemplated his next words. "We must protect Mary."

Alexander's brow furrowed. "Protect how?"

Nate took a deep breath, steeling himself. "I intend to ask for her hand in marriage. Immediately."

The silence that followed was deafening. Alexander's mouth dropped open. He lifted his brow and stared at Nate unblinking until his mouth curved into a slow smile. "You love her."

It wasn't a question.

Nate nodded, and a weight lifted from his chest at the admission. "I do. More than I can say."

"You have my blessing." Alexander stood slowly and extended his hand. "And my eternal gratitude for protecting her when I failed to do so."

Nate grasped Alexander's hand, and a surge of determination filled him. "I'm sure Mary will tell us what happened before I got there. But let me fill you in on what happened from when I arrived. She was in Blackwood's private box, alone with the cad. When I called out, she rushed out as pale as a ghost and somewhat dishevelled. Anyone could have seen that something wasn't right. Fortunately there were very few people about."

Nate took a breath. "Blackwood followed her out, and we had a somewhat tense exchange."

"Good." Alexander nodded his approval.

"By then, other people were coming into the corridor for the intermission, so Blackwood made himself scarce. But not before bumping into me and making some vague threat about it 'not being over'.

"The whole thing left a foul taste in my mouth, to be honest. I'm worried about what Blackwood meant, what he might do. I'm glad I was there to intervene when I did."

Alexander poured two brandies and handed one to Nate. "He's after her dowry, I'm sure of it. Money and connections to wealth and influence. He intended to compromise her, assuming that I would wed her to him."

Chapter Nine

Nate escorted Alexander and her back home after the theatre. When they arrived, Nate excused himself and followed Alexander to his study.

Mary could only guess what they discussed, but no doubt it had everything to do with Sebastian's unwelcome interest in her. She clenched her fists to stop her hands from trembling. Thank the heavens that no one had seen her confrontation with the odious man. She'd felt so safe with Nate. With her stomach tied in knots, she watched him disappear down the hallway.

Hawkins stood aside, waiting for her decision. "Is Lady Eleanor in her sitting room?"

"She is still with Lady Beatrice, I believe. The physician left a few moments ago."

There was no need to disturb Lady Beatrice's rest. She must have felt terrible asking for help to reach the retiring room. Mary thanked him and made her way to Alice's room.

Lady Alice was still in bed, not yet recovered from her illness, but her face lit up when Mary entered. She held out her hands in welcome.

"Mary! How was the theatre? You all seem to be home earlier than I expected."

"We left at the intermission." Mary sighed as she sat on the edge of the bed. "The evening has certainly been eventful."

Alice's perceptive gaze scrutinised Mary's face. "Well, don't keep me waiting. What has happened?"

Mary kicked off her shoes and curled her feet under her dress on the bed. "First, you were right, and the physician wrong. Lady Beatrice complained of stomach pains throughout the first half, then Alexander and Eleanor had to help her to the retiring room just before the interval started."

"I knew it! I only drank one glass of punch, and my bonnet shaded my face." Alice's face fell. "I'm so sorry Lady Beatrice is ill. Has the physician seen her?"

"I believe he left moments ago. Eleanor is with her now."

"What a shame you missed the second half of the—" Alice stopped mid-sentence and cupped Mary's cheek. "Don't cry, dearest. Please tell me, what is wrong."

Mary collapsed into Alice's arms, her body shaking with sobs she could no longer contain. The events of the evening crashed over her like a tidal wave, leaving her feeling raw and vulnerable. Alice held her close, gently stroking her back, offering silent comfort until Mary's sobs subsided into quiet sniffles.

"I'm sorry," Mary whispered, her voice rough from crying. "I've wet your robe." She accepted the handkerchief Alice offered and dabbed at her tear-stained cheeks.

"Don't be silly. It will dry." Alice's eyes filled with concern. The bell tinkled as she rang for service. "We will get tea. I still have to drink Cook's dreadful mixture." She gave a melodramatic shudder. "I'm sure she will send proper tea for you. Perhaps even some Madeleines she made today."

Despite herself, a weak smile tugged at Mary's lips. She could always depend on Alice to lighten the mood.

"We can share the cake." Mary sniffled again and delicately blew her nose. "I doubt you will want this handkerchief back."

"Goodness, no. I have a drawer of them."

"Is Cook's special tea so awful? She swears it cures all stomach ailments."

"Maybe it does. I asked what goes into it, and do you know what she said?"

Mary shook her head.

"She mentioned chamomile, peppermint, ginger, and fennel. I'm not sure they're all in the tea at once. She did not mention actual tea at all. I can tell you it tastes sweet, floral, minty, spicy, and like liquorice all at the same time. And not in a good way."

Mary laughed, just as Alice had meant.

Then Alice squeezed her hands. "No more procrastinating."

Mary started recounting the evening's events, her voice trembling. With some fear, yes, but also a healthy dose of indignation. Sebastian's leering face swam in her memory, her hands clenched into fists as her stomach churned. But then there was Nate... Brave, dependable Nate, coming to her rescue. The memory of his protective stance sent a flutter through her chest, a warmth that pushed back against the chill of fear.

Alice listened, her expressive face mirroring Mary's own emotions. Her eyes widened in shock at Blackwood's behaviour, and she gripped Mary's hand in support. But when Mary spoke of Nate, she caught a knowing glimmer in Alice's eyes.

"Nate is perfect for you, Mary." Alice's tone left no room for argument. "You are attracted to him. And he's kind, attentive, and clearly cares for you deeply, unlike that wretched Blackwood."

Heat rose in Mary's cheeks. Was it that obvious? "But what if I'm only imagining these feelings?" She whispered the words, voicing the doubt that gnawed at her. "What if I'm just grateful to Nate for saving me?"

Alice shook her head. "You know it's more than that. Goodness, you were hiding in that copse of trees at Lady Lamberts for ages." Her gaze narrowed. "You still haven't told me about that. Your eyes light up when you talk about him. And the way he looks at you? His feelings are undeniable."

Mary dropped her gaze to her lap, where she fidgeted with the fabric of her dress. There was more. A fear she'd been trying to push down since it happened. "There's something else," she admitted, her voice low. "I'm terrified, Alice. What if someone saw my confrontation with Blackwood? What if word gets out, and I become the subject of gossip?"

The words tumbled out, voicing the dread building inside her. "And Nate? What if his feelings change? If my reputation is tarnished, would he still..." She couldn't finish, the possibility too painful to voice.

Alice's hands closed over hers, warm and reassuring. "Oh, Mary." Her voice filled with a certainty Mary wished she could feel. "Nate isn't a man to be swayed by idle gossip. He knows your character, your heart. If anything, I believe this would only strengthen his resolve to protect and support you."

Mary wanted desperately to believe her. "Do you think so?"

"I do." Alice squeezed Mary's hands. "But more importantly, we won't let it come to that. Whatever comes, you're not alone in this, Mary. Remember that. You have your sisters, Alexander, and Nate and me, all in your corner."

Mary nodded, drawing a shaky breath. The fear was still there, a knot in her stomach that refused to unravel. But Alice offered much needed comfort. Whatever challenges lay ahead, at least she wouldn't have to face them alone. It wasn't much, but for now, it was enough to hold on to.

Chapter Ten

Nate accepted a delicate cup of sought-after Bohea tea from Eleanor. The smoky, malty scent filled his nostrils as he lifted it to his lips, the aroma mingling with the heady perfume of roses wafting through the open window. He took a sip, savouring the complex flavours dancing on his tongue, all the while acutely aware of Mary's presence across the room.

His heart had quickened at the sight of her. He longed to get Mary alone, to discern if her feelings matched his, but propriety was a cruel mistress. Politeness dictated he call at the appropriate hour and engage in the expected amount of small talk, no matter how much his heart yearned for more.

"I'm so glad you could join us today, Nate." Eleanor's eyes twinkled with mischief. She gestured to the array of sweet and savoury treats on the table, each one a miniature work of art. "You must try one of Cook's tea cakes. She has flavoured them with citrus and spices, and they are divine. I'm sure they could tempt St. Anthony to break his fast."

He plucked one of the tiny cakes from the platter, eyeing it with suspicion. He'd never had much of a sweet tooth and found most treats overly sweet. Steeling himself, he took a small bite. His eyes widened in surprise—Eleanor was right. The citrus and spice together pushed the sweetness into the background.

Mary giggled, the sound so full of light, Nate couldn't help but grin at her even though he had no idea what caused her mirth. The simple joy of her laughter brightened the room.

She covered her mouth with her hand and gave him a coy look. "Forgive me, Lord Everhart, you gave that tiny cake quite a glare before popping it in your mouth. I almost expected it to burst into flames under your scrutiny."

Emboldened by her teasing, he reached for another treat. "I might glower at this one, as well. One can never be too careful with these treacherous little confections."

He furrowed his brow, narrowed his eyes, and fixed the innocent cake with his most menacing scowl. Mary and Alice erupted into giggles, while Eleanor looked on with affectionate exasperation.

"Come now, you two. We all know that you call each other Nate and Mary." Alice nudged Mary, a conspiratorial grin on her face. "It's quite adorable. Little hearts should appear in the surrounding air."

Heat crept up his neck, but rather than embarrassment, pleasure filled him at the sight of Mary's rosy cheeks. With Blackwood's threats hanging over them, it was a relief to know she had such close friends nearby. He could even forgive Alice's determination to embarrass them both.

Nate cleared his throat and turned to Alice. "I am pleased to see you so well recovered, Lady Alice. May I ask how Lady Beatrice is faring?"

The cheerful atmosphere evaporated as Eleanor set down her cup with a clatter, the sound sharp in the sudden silence.

Nate scrambled to apologise. "Please forgive me, Lady Weston. I had no intention—"

"Dearest Nate, I insist you call me Eleanor." She dabbed at her lips with one of the soft linen napkins. Her tone was gentle, taking the sting out of her words. "Do not trouble yourself, your concern is most kind."

"She's still abed, Nate." Alice let out a heavy breath. "I fear I passed on an illness that lasted only two days for me but is much worse for Lady Beatrice. I feel dreadful about it."

"It wasn't your fault, you silly goose." Mary patted Alice's hand.

"The physician said an excess of yellow bile, or the London miasma caused the illness. More likely, it's that ghastly new perfume Lady Windermere insists on dousing herself in."

"That man is an old fool—"

"Alice, that is quite enough." Eleanor interjected in a tone that brooked no argument. "I assure you Nate, our physician is most capable and has assured us that Lady Beatrice will be fine after several days' rest. Girls, this is not appropriate discussion for the drawing room. Nate must think me the most ill-mannered of mentors. Whatever will he tell his brother, the Duke of Haversham, about the company he keeps?"

Alice and Mary both lowered their gazes to the carpet as they apologised, missing the exaggerated wink Eleanor threw Nate's way.

He played along and adopted an excessively proper tone. "I assure you, Lady Weston, that I shall inform my brother of nothing but the most refined conversation. Though I may have to omit the part about cake-glaring. He has little sense of humour, you see."

Sadly, that was quite the truth about his brother. But he didn't get time to lament his luck in the sibling stakes.

Mary's head snapped up, and their gazes connected. "Oh, Nate." Her voice filled with warmth. "Your brother needn't worry. Your glare is far too charming to be fearsome."

Nate chuckled. "Is that a compliment or an insult?"

"We would not dream of insulting you." Eleanor fluttered her lashes at him. "Well, now that we've established Nate's inability to intimidate baked goods, shall we move on to more pressing matters? Like whether he can juggle these teacakes? I've always thought a man's juggling skills were a true measure of his character."

The ladies laughed aloud, and Nate's grin stretched his cheeks. He may not have gotten Mary alone yet, but surrounded by warmth, laughter, and her radiant smile, the afternoon was perfect just as it was.

A knock at the door interrupted their gaiety. Hawkins entered with measured steps, a letter on a silver tray. "From the dowager countess and marked urgent, Your Grace." His impassive face betrayed a hint of concern. "I thought it wise to interrupt."

Eleanor's eyes widened. Fear flickered across her features as she reached for the letter from her mother. Alice and Mary gripped hands, watching in tense silence, the spectre of tragedy always near in childbirth.

With shaking fingers, Eleanor broke the seal, her breath catching as she unfolded the paper. The room held its breath as her gaze darted across the page. The tension broke as Eleanor let out a small, joyous squeal, her face transformed by relief and delight.

"Oh, thank heavens. Listen to this:"

"*Dearest Eleanor,*

"*Olivia has given birth after a long and difficult labour. There were moments of great fear, I confess, but thanks be to God, she is recovering well. She was delivered of two bonnie daughters, both beautiful and doing well.*

"*These precious little ones have already wrapped us all around their tiny fingers. Give Olivia a few days to rest, and then you must come and visit. Bring your sisters and Alice too. Caroline is so enamoured she scarcely wants to give the babes back to Olivia!*

"*With all my love, Mother.*"

Eleanor looked up, her eyes shining with unshed tears of joy and relief. Alice and Mary hugged one another in a chorus of delighted exclamations.

Mary reached out to clasp Eleanor's hand, her own eyes misting over. "Oh, Eleanor. What wonderful news! Twins, and both girls—how marvellous!"

A lump formed in Nate's throat, finding himself deeply moved by the palpable relief and happiness in the room.

"A cause for celebration, indeed." He raised his teacup in a small toast. "To Olivia and her daughters—may they have long and happy lives."

"I was so worried." Eleanor dabbed her eyes with a handkerchief. "When I saw that urgent letter... But now, such joy, such a blessing."

The room glowed with renewed warmth, laughter now mingled with a deeper happiness. United in relief and celebration, they formed a beautiful tableau of joy. He wasn't family yet, and this was their moment. A bittersweet pang signalled it was time to take his leave.

Mary walked him to the door, her hand resting lightly on his arm. The innocent touch stirred a longing within him—to belong, to marry and have his own family. He grinned at the thought of children running amok through his conservatory and greenhouses. Unfortunately, Hawkins hovered close by, a gentle reminder of propriety. After all, they weren't courting yet, let alone engaged. Pulling Mary aside for a private, heart-to-heart talk would be impossible. He grasped at the next best thing—a chaperoned outing.

"Have you visited Regent's Park yet?" The words tumbled out, almost of their own accord.

Mary gave him a full, radiant smile. It was as if a hidden lantern kindled within. Nate decided he would make it his mission to bring that smile to her face every day.

"Only once, and it was glorious. I would love to go again." Her cheeks flushed as she covered her mouth. "Forgive me, I didn't mean to suggest. Oh, my goodness. Please don't tell your brother."

Nate laughed, the sound rich with his affection. "Cross my heart, I will not mention a thing. Perhaps we could visit the gardens tomorrow. If Eleanor approves, of course, and we can find a suitable chaperone. It's a popular destination for courting couples—"

He broke off, realising the implications of his words. This wasn't how he planned to ask to court Mary.

Mary's breath caught, her eyes wide. "Is that what we are, Nate?"

Nate was speechless. He opened and closed his mouth like a goldfish. What a fool thing to say!

Yet, as Mary gazed at him with such hope and tenderness, he didn't feel foolish at all. Instead, he brought her hand to his lips to kiss her knuckles. "We could be, if it would please you."

A delightful blush bloomed on her cheeks, and she glanced down. "It would please me very much."

"Then let me know—"

"I'll ask Eleanor now." Mary darted back to the drawing room and returned with Eleanor in tow.

Eleanor raised her brow. "Are you planning a turn around the Avenue Gardens, a spot of boating, the Broad Walk, taking a picnic on the grass, or poking about in the greenhouses?"

"Can we do a picnic lunch?" Mary clasped her hands under her chin. "We need nothing formal or elaborate, just a blanket on the grass."

Nate's lips curved into a smile as he watched Mary, her eyes dancing with excitement. God, but her enthusiasm was infectious. Most young women he encountered seemed to speak from a memorised script, each word measured and weighed. But Mary? She wore her heart on her sleeve, her words tumbling out unfiltered and sincere. It felt like a gulp of fresh air after escaping a stuffy ballroom. He leaned in, drawn to her authenticity like a moth to a flame. When was the last time he'd met someone so genuine? He couldn't remember. The thought awakened a longing for authenticity he hadn't known he was missing.

Eleanor gazed at him with a playful smile on her lips. It hit him that he was yet to answer her question. "That was a disturbingly full list of potential activities at Regent's Park."

"I do like to be thorough. Alexander isn't needed in parliament tomorrow, so we will both attend and enjoy a day in the sun as well."

Mary grinned as if she'd just received the best gift in the world.

Nate straightened, a plan forming in his mind. "Might I suggest a picnic luncheon, followed by a stroll through the conservatories?" He met Mary's gaze, then Eleanor's. "If it pleases you ladies—and of course, Alexander—I would be delighted to make the arrangements. Shall we say one o'clock at the park's entrance?"

At Eleanor's agreement, he bowed to the sisters, now arm-in-arm on the porch, and strode to his waiting carriage with a jaunt in his step.

He arrived home to find his butler hovering at the door. "Watson?"

Watson gave a delicate cough. "A missive from your brother, I'm afraid. I had no choice but to read it as the boy demanded a return message."

Nate's good mood evaporated. "How have I displeased him this time?" Nate handed off his hat and gloves, determined to make it into his study.

"I am sure you will find out soon enough sir. He has asked you to present yourself at his Mayfair address as soon as possible."

Damn it, he'd just returned from Mayfair. A summons from his brother never promised good times, and ignoring it might bring the man to his doorstep at the worst time. "What message did you send back?"

"Just that you were out, and I did not expect you back until later."

"Well done, Watson. I think I've got time for one drink before scurrying into his domain."

Watson agreed and preceded him to the study to pour his drink.

An hour later, Nate found himself in his brother's opulent study, the Duke of Haversham's piercing gaze fixed upon him. The duke was ten years older and much like his father, while Nate had always felt closer to their mother. While Charles hunted and played war games, Nate drew pictures of wildflowers and collected seeds. Neither his father nor brother ever had anything good to say about him.

The tension in the room crackled like static before a storm. Neither greeted the other, both remained standing.

"Brother," the duke began, his voice cold and controlled. "I've heard some disturbing rumours about your recent associations."

Nate's jaw clenched. He already had an idea where this was heading, but this was one matter upon which he would not kneel before his brother. "Good afternoon, Charles. I trust you are well. What associations are those?"

"The Darrow girl." Charles' mouth twisted, as if the name itself left a foul taste in his mouth. "You are spending an inordinate amount of time in her company."

"Lady Mary is a delightful young woman." Nate pushed down rising anger and kept his voice even. "I cannot see how my friendship with her is any of your concern."

Charles narrowed his eyes. "It becomes my concern when it threatens our family's reputation. Her family courts scandal, and I'm hearing unsavoury rumours about her name."

A surge of anger coursed through Nate. He stepped closer to his brother. "Rumours? Explain."

"The kind that no respectable woman should be associated with." Charles jammed his arms across his chest, the vein in his temple throbbing. "I won't sully my lips by repeating them. She is not a suitable match for someone of your station."

Nate gritted his teeth and clenched his hands into fists at his sides. It wouldn't do to strangle the duke in his own study. "These rumours? Did you hear them from Blackwood or one of his cronies?"

The duke's silence was answer enough.

They were acquaintances, his brother and Blackwood. One of the many connections that Blackwood could use to harm Mary.

"For God's sake, Charles!" Nate's composure shattered. "Can't you see what's happening? Blackwood is trying to sabotage Mary's reputation because he can't stand the thought of losing."

Mary's dowry crossed his mind, but if Charles didn't already know, Nate wasn't about to enlighten him.

"Lower your voice," the duke hissed. "Whether or not the rumours are true is irrelevant. She carries a taint. That's all we need to know."

A wave of disgust washed over Nate. "You perpetuate this injustice? Cast aside an innocent young woman based on nothing but malicious gossip?"

"How do you know it's malicious—"

"Because I know Blackwood and I know Mary."

"Maybe you do, but I will protect our family name. Something you seem incapable of doing yourself."

The two brothers glared at each other, years of resentment and misunderstanding bubbling to the surface.

Nate spoke, his voice low and dangerous, "I will not abandon Mary based on unfounded rumours and your misplaced sense of family honour. If you wish to protect our name, perhaps you should start by not giving credence to every piece of slanderous gossip that crosses your path."

Nate turned on his heel and stormed out of the study and his childhood home, leaving his brother seething behind him.

The cool London air hit his warm skin but did nothing to cool his fury or cobble his determination. He would prove Mary's worth, not just to his brother, but to all of society if necessary.

Blackwood would pay for his underhanded tactics.

Chapter Eleven

Toast and tea forgotten, Mary's hands trembled as she clutched the latest edition of The Times, the thin paper crinkling under her tightening grip. She scanned the society pages with growing horror. How could this be happening? Just days ago, she had been strolling through Regent's Park with Nate, the scent of blooming flowers the perfect backdrop to the hope blooming in her chest. Now, her world was aflame and crumbling around her.

"...one wonders if an announcement regarding Lady Mary and Lord Everhart is imminent, or if the young lady's reputation is beyond salvaging..."

The words blurred as tears threatened to spill. Mary blinked them back, her throat constricting with the effort. She would not cry, not here, not now. But oh, how she wanted to flee, to hide away in her greenhouse where the plants didn't judge or whisper cruel falsehoods.

Unfortunately, her distress did not go unnoticed. The gentle clinking of porcelain ceased as the conversation between Eleanor and Lady Beatrice halted. Alexander's chair scraped harshly against the floor as he stood and pulled the paper from Mary's grasp.

"This is an outrage!" His voice boomed and echoed in Mary's head.

He slapped the paper onto the table in front of Eleanor, the sound sharp in the tense silence. "Who would dare spread such vicious lies?"

The vein at Alexander's temple pulsed, Eleanor's face drained of colour, and Lady Beatrice sat pale and rigid in her chair.

"Oh, my dear, I am so sorry."

Sorry? Mary's mind raced. What did Lady Beatrice have to be sorry for? Unless she had something to do with these rumours. No, she couldn't think like that. Lady Beatrice was just sorry that this had happened. She trusted her family implicitly.

The entry of Alice interrupted her spiralling thoughts. Alice traipsed to the breakfast table, her usually cheerful face pinched with worry. Dark circles under her eyes suggested a sleepless night.

"Eat your breakfast, Mary." Eleanor tapped her arm.

"I can't. I'm not hungry. May I be excused?"

"No," Alexander responded instead of Eleanor, his tone harsh. "You will not let this drivel affect your health."

"Just one piece of toast, dearest." Eleanor squeezed her hand. "You too, Alice. Then you may return to your rooms to dress for the day."

Mary closed her eyes against a sharp pain at her temple. What was the point of getting into a day dress? No one would visit. Not even Nate had answered her letters. The thought of him brought a fresh wave of anguish. Was he regretting their association now?

"No argument, Mary. Emily will bring you a chamomile tea." Eleanor used her big sister tone, one that brooked no opposition.

Mary just nodded and picked up the slice of toast she had buttered before she started reading the paper. The bread felt like sawdust in her mouth, but she forced herself to chew and swallow. The sooner she ate, the sooner she could escape their pitying scrutiny.

Alice followed her up the stairs. "Mary, I must speak with you. It's rather urgent."

In the privacy of Mary's bedchamber, Alice's words tumbled out in a rush. "I went for a walk this morning to clear my head, and goodness, this sounds idiotic, but I think someone followed me."

Mary's blood ran cold, her skin prickled with goose bumps. "Alice, what on earth is happening?"

"It could be a reporter, out to dig up more salacious gossip for that rag."

"It's not like you to rise so early. What's wrong?" Mary pressed, but Alice would not meet her gaze.

Alice's face turned crimson as she twisted her fingers in her robe. "It's nothing, just a slight head cold, that's all." She gave a small, unconvincing sniff.

Before Mary could challenge Alice and root out the cause of her embarrassment, Eleanor entered, a letter clutched in her hand, her knuckles almost translucent against the cream-coloured paper.

She swallowed. "It's from Olivia. James has been fielding strange inquiries about our family's finances. This can't be a coincidence."

Mary sank onto her bed, her mind whirling. The room seemed to tilt around her. "Blackwood." She whispered the name, tasting bitterness on her tongue. "It must be him. He threatened us after all, and he was so angry after... after the incident. But why? What could he hope to gain?"

As if summoned by her thoughts, a footman appeared with a note. Mary's heart leapt as she recognized Nate's handwriting. She tore it open and drank in his words.

My dearest Mary,

I have missed you these past few days and apologise for my absence.

Unfortunately, I have made some troubling discoveries. Blackwood is in dire financial straits. His father's poor investments and gambling debts have left his family estate in need of expensive repairs. He's been asking questions about the Darrow family finances and the Weston fortune. And specific questions about your dowry.

I'll be back soon. Please be careful. I couldn't bear it if anything happened to you.

Yours always, Nate

Mary pressed the letter to her chest, warmth blooming despite the ominous news. Nate cared for her, truly cared. She could admit how deeply her own feelings ran. If only circumstances were different... But what did it matter now? They could not wed, not even make any announcements. The Times was right. Her reputation was beyond salvaging, but Nate's was not. If he withdrew his suit, he could walk away clean and free.

The thought of losing Nate, of living her life without him, sent a wave of pain through her so intense, it was almost physical. Not even her beloved greenhouse, her sanctuary of peace and growth, could entice her to live again if he were gone.

Her tears flowed, and she let Eleanor and Alice think she was crying about the news they had received this morning. She could not bear to voice her fears about Nate and the future that now seemed impossibly out of reach. Instead, she curled into herself on the bed, letting sobs wrack her body as Eleanor gently stroked her hair and Alice held her hand. The three of them united in their worry and grief.

The following evening, Mary stepped into Lady Harrington's musicale and immediately felt the weight of countless gazes upon her. Whispers followed in her wake, and more than one matron made a show of moving their daughters away as if her mere presence could taint them with scandal. The sting of their judgment pressed against her chest, squeezing her heart with its invisible hand. She lifted her chin, determined not to let them see how much it hurt. Had she ever faced worse? But it never stopped cutting.

Each snide glance, each cruel whisper, chipped away at her carefully constructed composure.

She wouldn't let them break her, but it felt as if the ground had already crumbled beneath her feet.

"Courage, my dear," Eleanor murmured, squeezing her hand with reassuring warmth. "Anyone that matters is on your side."

Anyone that matters? The words felt hollow. How could Eleanor be so sure? Mary glanced around the room. It seemed everyone of influence in attendance apart from Alexander and Nate had already passed their verdict and found her wanting. They didn't see her, they only saw a scandal in the making, one that clung to her like a shadow.

She had done nothing wrong, yet here she was, the subject of gossip and derision.

The first notes of a pianoforte sonata filled the air, and for a moment, the tightness across her shoulder eased, the music wrapping around her like a soothing balm. She clung to the reprieve, letting the melody drown out the murmurs, trying to lose herself in the gentle rhythm. Would she be lucky enough to escape reality for long?

Her gaze landed on Lady Beatrice, almost hidden by a potted palm, engaged in what appeared to be a tense conversation with Blackwood. Even from across the room, Lady Beatrice's pallor was obvious, as was the way her lips pressed into a thin line, and she clutched her walking stick like a lifeline.

A knot of worry tightened in her stomach. She nudged Eleanor. "Look at Lady Beatrice. Something's not right."

She started at a fast pace toward Lady Beatrice, but a gentleman approached, cutting her off. His face sparked a vague memory from her first ball, not that she could remember his name. It felt like a lifetime ago. That young, innocent girl, untouched by scandal, was long gone. Sometimes she barely recognised herself anymore.

He bowed over her hand, his demeanour earnest. "Lady Mary." His voice was soft, almost sad. "Might I have a word in private? It's regarding a matter of some delicacy."

Every instinct screamed at Mary to outright refuse and send him on his way. The last thing she needed was another "delicate" conversation, another veiled insult cloaked in feigned politeness. But years of ingrained etiquette made her hesitate. "I... that is..."

"Spare me a moment, my lady. What I must share is not fit for polite company."

Panic clawed at her core. She swallowed hard. It was imperative to maintain her composure in front of so many eyes.

"Mary!" Alice's voice cut through her indecision. "I believe Lady Beatrice is looking for you. Something about the next performance?"

Relief flooded through Mary. "I'm so sorry, sir, but I'm needed elsewhere. Perhaps another time?"

As she turned to leave, she caught sight of Nate striding towards them, his expression thunderous. The nameless gentleman paled and melted into the crowd.

Her heart skipped a beat. She hadn't realised Nate would be in attendance. Eleanor had insisted that she come, arguing that hiding in her room would just fuel the ton's gossip. Not that her presence seemed to have helped anything. In fact, she felt more exposed than ever, raw and vulnerable under the scrutiny.

Nate's expression softened as he reached her, morphing into the look she had come to cherish. He gripped her hand, his voice low and urgent. "What did he say to you?"

Her breath caught at the intensity in his gaze. Propriety be damned. She pressed closer to him, their joined hands against his chest. "Nothing of importance." She gulped, adrenaline from the encounter still coursing through her veins. "Thanks to Alice's timely interruption, it was nothing but more insinuations."

Nate's jaw tightened, a fierce protectiveness in his gaze. "He won't bother you again. I can promise you that."

How could he be so sure? The question rose on her lips and died there. She wouldn't burden him further, not when he was only dragged into this mess because of her. She lay her hand on his arm, appreciating his strength. She had to tell him about Blackwood accosting Lady Beatrice. "I'm worried about Lady Beatrice. She was talking to Blackwood earlier and looked upset."

Before Nate could respond, a hush fell over the room. Lady Harrington strode toward Eleanor, her face a mask of cold politeness. "Lord and Lady Weston, I'm afraid I must ask for your party to leave. She glared at Mary. "Your presence is causing some discomfort among my other guests."

The words hit Mary like a slap. They were being cast out like lepers.

Her mind spun. Too many thoughts battled for dominance. Shame, anger, helplessness. Each one tugged hard, but beneath it all, a hollow ache settled in her chest. How had it come to this? She had lived by society's rules, only to have them turn against her and her whole family.

Alexander stepped forward, his eyes blazing with controlled fury. "Lady Harrington." His voice cut through the tension. "It is a pity when the virtues of hospitality and kindness are discarded in favour of pettiness and prejudice."

Lady Harrington's expression flickered, but Alexander continued, undeterred, "Mary has done nothing to deserve such treatment. You and your guests should feel discomfort for shunning an innocent young lady based on unfounded gossip. Good evening."

Alexander and Eleanor strode to the doors with their heads held high, dignity intact despite the humiliation. Mary took Nate's arm, her grip tight as she fought tears that threatened to fall. There wasn't much she could do but follow her sister's example. Each step felt like an eternity. If whispers and stares could burn, a brand would have etched into her back.

Not a single soul came forward to bid them farewell.

"Lady Alice, wait!" It was Lord Lynden, Alice's favourite suitor. He hurried towards them, his face a picture of distress.

Alice turned, her eyes bright. "My lord, please. I beg you, go back inside. I couldn't bear it if your reputation suffered because of me." Her voice trembled, betraying the fear and anguish she was trying so hard to hide.

Lord Lynden took her hand and pressed a tender kiss to her fingers. "I will not embarrass you further here, my love. I will call on you tomorrow." He kissed her hand again before reluctantly retreating, the parting clearly as painful for him as it was for Alice.

A hole tore in Mary's heart, a searing pain spreading through her chest like fire. Alice cared for him—perhaps a good deal more than she had let on, and she might lose him. Guilt crashed over her in relentless waves. She had never felt more like a burden than in the moment.

"Oh, Alice." Mary whispered. "I'm so sorry. This is all my fault."

Alice gripped her hand, her gaze unwavering. "Don't you dare blame yourself, Mary Althea Darrow. We're in this together, come what may."

Conflicting emotions rushed through Mary. Guilt battling with the deep sadness settled in her chest. But beneath it all was an unshakable love for her family and for Nate, who even now had not let go of her arm, grounding her with his solid presence. She squeezed Alice's hand back, drawing strength from her unwavering support.

They stepped out into the cool night air, and Mary drew in a long breath. She let the crisp air fill her lungs, but it did little to douse the fire in her chest. Nate deserved better than this.

She had to let him go.

"Nate, you must leave me now." The words felt like bitter stones on her tongue, each syllable a betrayal of everything she wanted. "Already it might be too late to—"

Before she could finish, Nate pulled her close, his hand cradling her cheek with a tenderness that made her breath catch.

He kissed her, softly at first, testing, asking a question she didn't know how to answer. On instinct, her lips parted, a quiet surrender. The moment his tongue brushed against hers, the world shifted beneath her feet.

A gasp escaped her, lost in the warmth of his mouth as he deepened the kiss. She tangled her fingertips in the curls at the nape of his neck, pulling him closer, as if she could melt into him entirely. Each tentative exploration of his mouth sent a tremor through her, a sensation so new and overwhelming it left her breathless.

How could a kiss do this? It wasn't just her lips. Warmth ignited from her core and radiated out. Heat spread to her fingertips and toes until her whole body throbbed with a need she knew only Nate could satisfy. She felt alive in a way she did not know was possible.

The world seemed to stop for a heartbeat. The whispers of the ton, the disapproving stares—all of it faded into the background. For a fleeting moment, there was only Nate. The taste of him, the solidity of his body against hers, and the way his hands held her as though she were something precious, something worth fighting for.

She had never felt safer than in his arms, and yet never more vulnerable. There was no hiding from him. He had laid her soul bare. The thought both terrified and thrilled her.

When they pulled apart, reality came crashing back as Eleanor's knowing smile, Alice's grin, and Lady's Beatrice's deep frown.

Heat climbed across Mary's face until even her ears burned. Dear Lord, what had she done?

Alexander lifted his brow, his expression unreadable as he clasped Nate on the shoulder. "I expect an offer on the table by the morning, my friend."

Mary's heart leapt into her throat. An offer? The idea had lingered at the edge of her mind since meeting Nate, but spoken aloud, it felt too real. Too soon. The timing was wrong, so wrong.

"You will have it," Nate replied without hesitation.

"No, Nate, Alexander. No, please, not like this." Mary gripped Nate's arm hard. Panic seized her, her lips still throbbing, her thoughts a tangled mess. "Please, let us clear my name first."

Alexander glared at her. "Marrying will clear your name, as at least half of the gossip focuses on your shenanigans with this man." He pointed at Nate. "We will gather to share everything we know and plan a counterattack. Did you bring your carriage, Nate?"

"I rode. I will wait for you at your townhouse."

Before Mary could protest further, Nate kissed her again—this time chastely on her cheek, before striding away.

The tenderness in his touch left her aching for more. Part of her wanted to reach out, to stop him from leaving. But in her mind, a nagging voice told her again, she had no right to drag his name through the mud.

She had to protect him, even from herself.

Mary sat as stiff as a board in the drawing room at Weston House. The familiar scents of beeswax and lavender did little to soothe her frayed nerves. The family had gathered, still dressed in their evening finery, the atmosphere tense and heavy with unspoken words. Even Hawkins, their ever-stoic butler, seemed more highly strung than usual. He supervised the delivery of the tea trolley, then pulled the door shut behind him.

Eleanor broke the oppressive quiet. "Shall I pour? We have tea or coffee—"

Mary could not stay quiet a moment longer. "Eleanor, I'm so sorry. So sorry—"

Eleanor pointed at her with the teaspoon she was holding. "Not another word. None of this is your fault."

Alexander strode to the drinks cabinet. "Brandy, Nate?"

"Thank you, yes."

"Sherry, ladies?"

"Clear heads are called for. The ladies will stick with tea and coffee." Lady Beatrice sat straight-backed in her preferred chair close to the fire.

Mary wasn't about to ride roughshod over Alexander's grandmother's decree, but she wouldn't have minded a fortifying sip to get her through this family meeting.

Lady Beatrice tapped her cane on the floor to get their attention. "There's something I must tell you all." Her voice quavered.

Nate took the brandy glass from Alexander, his expression grim. "Mary also has something to share, as do I."

Mary swallowed. "It's nothing to worry about. But yes, I do, and Alice too."

Alice stared at the rug at her feet. "Mine isn't too terrible either."

Alexander glanced at his grandmother and drew a long breath. "Mary, Alice, Nate, tell us what we need to know. I think Grandmother's secret will need another brandy."

Lady Beatrice gave a brief nod and relaxed a little.

Nate settled beside Mary, the warmth of his presence a great comfort.

She clasped her hands in her lap. "Earlier this evening, a gentleman approached me." The memory of his unsettling earnestness sent a shiver down her spine. "I remember dancing with him at the Carlisle's ball, but I can't recall his name. His manner was disconcerting." She took a breath and chose her words with care. "He spoke like an actor, trying too hard to get his lines just right.

She couldn't stop knotting her fingers in her lap, the fine muslin of her gown crumpling beneath them. "He requested a word in private, mentioning a matter of some delicacy. When I hesitated, he pressed further, insisting that it was not something fit for polite company."

A flush of shame heated Mary's cheeks as she recalled her momentary temptation to hear him out. "Thank heavens Alice intervened when she did."

"Who the devil was it?" Sitting opposite his grandmother, Alexander smacked his palm onto the arm of his chair.

She whacked her cane against his calf. "Alexander, language."

"Whittington, I believe," Nate responded. "I will be speaking with him tomorrow."

"Make sure you do."

"What on earth could he mean by 'matter of some delicacy'?" Alice's face shone pale in the fire and candlelight.

"A friend of Blackwood's, damn him to hell. He meant nothing." Alexander hastened to move his ankles out of his grandmother's reach. "It was a ruse to pull Mary into a compromising situation. Blackwood has gone too far this time. Alice?"

Alice repeated her story about being followed, and her belief it could have been a reporter.

Alexander's anger flared again. "Neither of you will leave the house alone. If neither Nate nor I are available, take a footman or two with you." He strode to the drinks cabinet again to pour fresh libations for himself and Nate.

"Forgive me, Grandmother," Eleanor said. "I believe a sherry would be most welcome."

Once everyone held a glass of fortifying spirits, their gazes turned to Nate.

"My brother, the duke." Nate's posture could not have been tighter.

Mary's heart constricted. This wasn't the first time Nate tensed up when mentioning his brother. She longed to offer comfort, to smooth away the tension on his face, yet decorum held her back.

"He demanded my presence to inform me he heard some disturbing rumours about my association with Lady Mary."

Nate's jaw clenched. There must have been so many words spoken that he couldn't bear to repeat. Mary couldn't stand it anymore. She leaned closer to him and took his free hand between her own.

"I'm afraid my brother and Blackwood are more than acquaintances. It started with Blackwood fagging for Charles at Eton, but it turned into more of a friendship despite their difference in ages. Charles claims he has heard unsavoury rumours about Mary, and he didn't deny they came from Blackwood."

Alexander's nose flared as his face flushed. But he circled his fingers, telling Nate to continue.

"There isn't much else to tell. He refused to specify what rumours Blackwood has instigated. No doubt, the blackguard still has hopes of riding in to rescue Mary with an offer of marriage after everyone else turns their backs on her."

Mary dropped her head into her hands. The very foundations of her world were crumbling beneath her feet. More tears pricked at her eyes, though whether they were tears of sorrow, shame, or raw anger, it was difficult to tell. Eleanor tried to pull her into a hug, but Mary resisted.

"Nate, you must not break with your family because of me." The words tasted bitter on her tongue. In truth, she wanted nothing more than to cling to him, propriety be hanged. "I couldn't bear it—"

Nate knelt before her. "Mary, my love, we will marry. If you would rather wait until after we clear your name, then we will wait. But not for too long, because I couldn't bear it, and I would trade my brother for you in a heartbeat."

His declaration of love and loyalty stirred something fierce within Mary. She gripped his hands and found the courage to refuse to give into tears, fear, or the shame and guilt that swirled within.

Lady Beatrice gave a delicate cough. Nate returned to sit beside Mary on the sofa, this time close enough for her to feel his leg next to hers.

"I believe it is my turn." In the glow of firelight, Lady Beatrice looked her age and more. "Blackwood knows a secret. A secret about our family that could ruin us if it ever came to light. He's been using it to pressure me, trying to gain my support for his pursuit of Mary. I have resisted thus far, but his hints are becoming more threatening."

Mary gasped. "Lady Beatrice, why didn't you tell us?"

"I was ashamed," the older woman whispered. "And afraid. But I see now that my silence has only made things worse. I apologise, grandson, I should have come to you as soon as that devil approached me.

Alexander frowned, his face darkening with anger. "What secret could he know that gives him such power over you?"

Lady Beatrice took a deep breath, her hands trembling. "Years ago, before you were born, your grandfather made a grievous mistake. He gambled away a significant portion of the family fortune. To cover the debt, he forged documents to claim a large inheritance from a distant relative who had no living heirs. It was a scandalous act, and if it were discovered, our family's reputation would be destroyed."

A chill ran down Mary's spine as her eyes widened in shock. She glanced at Nate, whose jaw clenched, the muscles in his face taut with barely contained fury. Alice's hand flew to her mouth, her eyes wide with disbelief. Eleanor's face paled, her usual calm shattered by the revelation.

Alexander tightened his fists at his sides, his body rigid with anger. "He's thought of this for some time. I would bet he has been waiting for a relative of mine to make her debut, and this year he was lucky enough to have a choice of Mary or Alice. By targeting Mary, he gets immediate access to her dowry, as well as both the Weston family fortune and the Duke of Wallingford's social credibility. When did he first approach you, Grandmother?"

"I am sorry to say it was weeks ago, weeks before the Carlisle's ball." She slumped even further. "If only I'd told you straight away, perhaps we could have avoided this nastiness."

"I doubt it." Alexander clenched his jaw. "He would just have pressured me. He still has the ledger and the evidence of Grandfather's perfidy."

"How did Blackwood find out about this?" Mary couldn't stop the quiver in her voice. It wasn't just a mistake, Alexander's grandfather had committed a grievous crime. Would the Weston family have to relinquish their considerable fortune?

Lady Beatrice's eyes filled with regret. "His father used the same lawyer. When he passed away and the practice closed, a clerk included several other files in the box that were returned to the Blackwood family. Unfortunately, the cretin found the forged documents in an old ledger your grandfather kept. He has threatened to expose the truth unless I support his suit for Mary's hand."

The room erupted in a chorus of voices, panic, and anger intertwining as everyone seemed to find something to say about the situation. But Mary's heart pounded with a singular, terrifying realisation. This wasn't just about her. He was targeting not just her, but her entire family—their reputation, their fortune, everything they held dear. A cold weight settled over her, the noose of Blackwood's blackmail tightening with each second.

She scanned the room, her gaze resting on the faces of those she loved—Alexander's fierce protectiveness, Eleanor's quiet strength, Alice's unwavering loyalty, and Nate... dear Nate, who had become her anchor in the storm. His presence gave her courage she never knew she possessed. Each one of them wore expressions of shock and resolve, their love for each other unspoken but deeply felt.

Mary gripped a spoon, its cool metal grounding her as she tapped it to get everyone's attention. "We will face this together." The strength and clarity in her voice surprised even her. "Blackwood may think he has the upper hand, but he has underestimated the strength of our family and the lengths we will go to protect one another."

As she spoke the words, her gaze met Nate's. His gaze softened, and he gave her a small, reassuring smile. She smiled back, knowing with absolute certainty that though trials lay ahead, their love would see them through.

Before the family could continue the conversation, Hawkins entered with a small silver tray. "Forgive me, sir, Lord Blackwood left this card. I tried to detain him, but he left before I could raise the alarm. He suggested a degree of urgency to bring it to you."

Alexander motioned him over and took the card. He tore it open, his brows knitting together as he read the brief message. In silence, he passed the note to Nate.

Mary leaned closer to read it, and her stomach twisted.

"Mary, what does it say?" Eleanor demanded.

Mary took a deep breath and voiced the horrid message from memory. *"A graceful exit, Lady Mary. Let's see if you can manage the same for your family next time."*

The room seemed to freeze, the silence almost suffocating. Blackwood hadn't finished with them. Far from it.

Mary straightened her spine. She didn't know what they could do, but her resolve hardened. "We will not back down. Blackwood started this game, but we will end it."

Chapter Twelve

The drawing room at Weston House was awash with afternoon sunlight and the thick scent of blooms and beeswax. Mary inhaled deeply, savouring the familiar scents. The gentle coos of newborn babies mingled with the rustle of silk gowns as her sisters moved about the room. For the first time in months, all four Darrow sisters were gathered, and Mary's heart swelled with a bittersweet mixture of joy and anxiety.

Cradling one of Olivia's twins in her arms, Mary marvelled at the infant's tiny fingers and rosebud lips. The weight of the baby, warm and trusting against her chest, stirred a longing in her that she hadn't expected. She found herself dreaming of her own family, of Nate holding their child, and the thought both thrilled and terrified her. With everything happening, would such a future even be possible?

"She has your nose, Olivia." Mary traced the baby's delicate features with a soft fingertip.

Olivia, resplendent in a flowing muslin gown that did little to hide her post-pregnancy figure, smiled from her armchair. "Everyone says so, though I swear I see more of James in them."

"They're perfect, Olivia. You must be so proud." The clink of fine bone china punctuated Eleanor's words as she poured tea, the familiar ritual a comfort amidst the tumult of Mary's emotions.

From her perch near the window, Caroline bounced her knee. "When can I hold one? I've been waiting for ages!"

Caroline's impatience reminded Mary of herself not so long ago, always eager to be treated as a grown woman.

"Patience, Caro," Eleanor chided gently. "Babies aren't playthings."

Caroline's face fell. "You know that Olivia let me hold them when they were hours old."

Mary felt a pang of sympathy for her youngest sister. She remembered all too well the frustration of being treated like a child when she longed to be seen as a woman.

As if reading Mary's thoughts, Caroline turned to her. "Mary, do you have any events to attend this week?"

Before Mary could respond, Eleanor interjected, "You know Mary can't accept invitations, given the circumstances."

A heavy silence fell over the room, pressing down on Mary like a physical weight. She felt the heat of her sisters' gazes upon her. The baby in her arms squirmed as if sensing her unease, and Mary forced herself to take a deep, calming breath.

Olivia broke the tension. "Oh, come now, Ellie. Not accepting a single invitation is going overboard."

"Overboard?" Eleanor's eyebrows shot up, her voice rising in pitch. "Need I remind you of the delicate situation in which we find ourselves? Mary must be cautious."

Mary's heart clenched at the reminder of her predicament. She sighed. "Eleanor is right, Olivia. Maybe it wouldn't matter if I hadn't met Nate, but I can't deny my feelings for him."

At the mention of her beau's name, a warmth spread through Mary's chest, battling with the cold fear that had taken residence there since the scandal had broken. She thought of his kind eyes, his gentle touch, the way he looked at her as if she were the only person in the world. How could something that felt so right be cause for such worry?

Olivia's eyes lit up. "Oh, do tell us more! Is he as handsome as Caroline tells me? As gallant?"

"Caroline, what have you been telling Olivia? This isn't one of your novels," Eleanor warned.

Olivia leaned forward, a mischievous glint in her eye. "No, it's better than any fiction. Come, Mary, regale us with tales of your dashing lord."

Mary felt her cheeks warm. "He's... wonderful. Kind and intelligent, and he understands me in a way no one else does."

"It's so romantic." Caroline sighed.

Eleanor set down her teacup with a sharp clink. "Romance is all well and good, but we must consider the practical implications. Mary, you must remember to be more guarded in your interactions with Lord Everhart. The ton is watching your every move."

"Oh, Ellie." Olivia settled a twin on her shoulder. "You sound positively ancient. Times are changing. Mary should follow her heart."

"That's easy for you to say," Eleanor retorted. "You're safely married to a duke. The rest of us don't have that luxury."

Olivia's eyes flashed. "Are you implying I married James for his title?"

"Of course not," Eleanor backpedalled, "but you can't deny your position affords you certain freedoms."

"Freedoms?" Olivia laughed bitterly. "You have no idea the pressures I face as a duchess."

Mary watched her older sisters bickering, a knot forming in her stomach as the discussion grew heated.

"This is precisely why I should have my season now!" Caroline burst out. "Why should I wait when clearly age doesn't guarantee a smooth debut?"

The two oldest sisters turned to the youngest. Guilt gnawed at Mary for all the trouble she had caused.

"Caroline!" Eleanor gasped. "That's an entirely inappropriate thing to say."

"Is it?" Caroline challenged. "Mary's facing scandal, Olivia married in haste, and you, Ellie... well, we all remember your garden escapade with Alexander."

A tense silence fell over the room. Mary was torn between amusement at Caroline's audacity and horror at the can of worms she'd opened.

"I believe." Olivia grinned. "Our little sister has a point."

"Don't encourage her." Eleanor stamped her foot. "Caroline, you're far too young—"

"I'm seventeen! The same age you were during your first season, Ellie."

"Times were different then," Eleanor argued.

"Exactly." Caroline pounced on the words. "Times are always changing, aren't they? So why cling to outdated traditions?"

Mary, sensing the situation spiralling out of control, tried to intervene. "Perhaps we should all take a breath—"

"Stay out of this, Mary." Eleanor and Olivia turned and glared at her.

"Don't speak to her like that." Caroline jumped back into the conversation. "Mary's the one in the thick of it. If anyone understands the challenges of navigating society, it's her."

Mary's patience finally snapped. "Enough! All of you." Her raised voice startled the baby in her arms, who began to whimper. "Oh, darling, I'm so sorry." She rocked the infant gently.

The simple act of soothing the baby calmed her own frayed nerves, reminding her of what truly mattered. The sudden cry broke the spell of anger that had fallen over the sisters. They all watched as Mary soothed the baby, their faces softening.

"Look at us," Olivia said quietly. "Squabbling like children when we should be celebrating."

Eleanor sighed, her shoulders slumping. "You're right. I'm sorry, all of you. I just worry."

"We know, Ellie," Mary said gently. "We all do, in our own ways."

Caroline approached hesitantly. "I'm sorry too. I shouldn't have said those things. I just feel so ready. And watching all of you, I'm afraid of missing my chance."

Olivia held out her arms, and Caroline went to her, accepting a warm embrace. "Oh, Caro. Your time will come, I promise. And when it does, you'll have three sisters to guide you through every step."

"Four sisters," Mary corrected with a smile. "Don't forget our dear cousin, Alice, who I'm sure will be married to Lord Lynden before too long."

They all laughed, the tension finally broken.

As the laughter subsided, Eleanor spoke up, "Maybe we've all been a bit set in our ways. Caroline, while I still think you're too young for a full season, perhaps we can discuss allowing you to attend a few smaller gatherings."

Caroline's face lit up. "Really?"

Eleanor nodded. "Really. I will speak to Mother and Lady Beatrice. And Mary." She turned to her younger sister. "I'm sorry if I've been overbearing. I trust your judgment, truly."

Love and warmth filled Mary's chest. "Thank you, Ellie. That means more than you know."

As the sisters settled into a more harmonious conversation, Mary looked around the room, her heart full. They may argue and disagree, but at the end of the day, the bond between the Darrow sisters was unbreakable.

Chapter Thirteen

Nate's pulse quickened as he approached the imposing façade of the Weston townhouse. It had been three days since he had seen Mary, and he missed her. A chill in the air nipped at his cheeks, a welcome distraction from the knot of anticipation tightening in his chest. He paused at the top of the steps, adjusting his cravat with fingers steadier than his nerves.

He'd visited Alex here countless times, but this was different. For the first time he'd be under the same roof as Mary, welcomed into the heart of her family.

The door swung open, and the warmth of the house—soft laughter, the murmur of voices, the scent of beeswax candles and fresh flowers mingling in the air—immediately enveloped him. Hawkins' impassive face did little to settle the storm brewing within.

"Your hat and cane, my lord." Hawkins winced before smoothing his expression again, his voice almost inaudible over the sudden, piercing wail of an infant.

Nate fumbled with his belongings, his nerves jangling at the thought of facing the formidable Darrow family, all of them assembled and watching, assessing his worth as a suitor for Mary. A blur of muslin and ribbons darted past him—a young girl, her face alight with curiosity as she raced toward the source of the infant's cry.

At the threshold of the drawing room, he paused, seeking Mary among the gathered faces. Instead, his gaze fell upon Olivia, the Duchess of Wallingford now, radiant in a gown of deep burgundy silk.

"Nate Everhart." Her voice was rich with amusement as she rose to greet him, offering her cheek for a kiss. "You are a dark horse, indeed. I didn't know you held such affection for my dear sister."

Her words struck like a well-aimed arrow. He straightened, willing his voice to stay steady. "Your Grace, it is wonderful to see you after so many months. It is honest to say that I was not yet aware of Mary's loveliness when you and I last saw one another. Though I assure you, my affection for Mary is very real now."

She smacked his arm playfully, her laugh light and genuine. "You better look after her, or you will have three Darrow sisters and two husbands on your tail like leeches." Her tone softened, genuine warmth in her gaze. "No more 'Your Gracing.' We've known each other for ages, and you will soon become as a brother to me."

"Olivia." He gave her a quick nod, relief washing over him at her serene acceptance. "Leeches sound horrid. But I have nothing to fear on that count, as I will worship Mary as she deserves."

James, the Duke of Wallingford, boomed out a laugh, his rich baritone resonating. "The Darrow sisters have a way of getting beneath your skin."

James cradled one twin in his arms, and his usually stern expression softened. The babe's tiny fist curled around his finger.

Nate approached, extending his hand. "Your Grace, it's a pleasure to see you again."

James shook his hand, his gaze appraising. "Lord Everhart, good to see you. I agree with Olivia. No more 'Your Gracing.' Alex tells me you will be part of the family soon." He lowered his voice, a hint of steel beneath the civility. "Thank you for supporting Mary. We stand united in clearing her name."

Nate inclined his head as the weight of the responsibility he felt settled on his shoulders. "I will do everything in my power to ensure we restore her honour."

More family gathered in the drawing room, lively chatter filling the air. The family passed the twins from one to another, their cherubic faces eliciting coos of delight. Olivia introduced him to Charlotte, James's daughter from his first marriage. The young girl curtsied and shook his hand with a gravity that belied her years.

The Dowager Countess Darrow sat with Lady Beatrice in front of the fire, their heads bent low in conversation, though their sharp eyes missed nothing.

And then she entered the room—Mary, with her youngest sister Caroline by her side. The sight of her sent a jolt through him, his breath catching in his throat. She was sunshine itself, her face lit as she greeted her new nieces with a burst of adorable baby sounds that seemed to echo in his very soul. Her gaze found his, and for a moment, the world narrowed to just him and Mary. She offered him a soft, shy smile that stirred something deep within him, a fierce, undeniable need to protect her, to claim her as his own.

The door opened to admit more tea and cakes, followed by Lady Abigail and her son, Caleb, the illegitimate offspring of Lord Darrow, never acknowledged by his father, but drawn into the wider family now. Mary rose to greet them and soon pulled the little boy to the seat next to her and introduced him to the twin girls.

The sight of her cradling one twin, surrounded by Charlotte and Caleb, filled him with a longing so intense it came close to overwhelming him. He had to be part of this. He had to make her his.

Mary stood to return a crying twin to her mother. While the room buzzed with family chatter, he made his way to her side. "I can see how pleased you are to be reunited with your family."

"I am. We four sisters were never apart until Olivia left us to look after Charlotte."

"And now she has returned a duchess."

"She wears it well." Mary smiled in Olivia's direction. Then, with a sudden spark in her eyes, she reached for Nate's hand, her fingers curling around his, sending a jolt of heat through his veins. "Come with me. I have something to show you."

"Should we..." Nate's mind scrambled to catch up, blood rushing south as she tugged him from the room. Whatever he had meant to say vanished, lost in the surge of desire that coursed through him. Perhaps a chaperone, or lack of one, but the thought slipped away.

Mary led him to the conservatory at the back of the house.

Nate stepped inside, the warm, humid air enveloping him, the rich tapestry of greenery and the heady scent of blooming flowers intoxicating his senses.

"Mary, what a lovely orchid!" He approached the showy plant on a pedestal in the middle of the room, his voice filled with genuine admiration. "Is that a Phalaenopsis? The blooms are spectacular."

Mary grinned up at him, her hand still resting on his arm, every movement of her fingers sending little shocks of awareness through his body. "I knew you'd appreciate it. It's from Loddiges Nursery in Hackney."

"I've made many purchases there myself. They have an impressive selection. Look at these petals." He moved closer, his breath mingling with hers as they both leaned in to admire the flower. "So delicate and almost translucent. The colours are exquisite—white with a touch of pink and those striking magenta spots."

"I love the way the blooms glow with an ethereal light, suspended like moths in mid-flight." Her voice was soft, almost reverent, as she wrapped her arms around his, pulling him even closer. Her touch, so natural and yet so intimate, sent his heart racing. "It enchanted me when I saw it in their catalogue, but it's even more beautiful in person. The way the petals fan out like moth wings is just mesmerising."

"Hence the common name, 'Moth Orchid.' They resemble a moth in flight." Nate's voice softened as he kissed the top of her head, his lips brushing against the soft strands of her hair. It was a brief, almost hesitant touch, but it still sent a shiver of pleasure down his spine. She leaned into him, her warmth seeping through his shirt. "You've done a splendid job with it, Mary. The blooms look very healthy."

"Thank you, Nate. Coming from you, that means a lot." Her cheeks flushed and her eyes sparkled with a mixture of pride and something else —something that sent his pulse racing. She hesitated, her gaze dropping to their joined hands before she spoke again. "I placed it where it gets plenty of indirect light, and I've been misting it to keep it humid."

"Perfect conditions for a Phalaenopsis." Nate admired not just her botanical prowess, but the way she had so effortlessly captured his heart. The more he learned about her, the deeper he fell. And he didn't want to do a damn thing about it. "They will thrive in this environment. And the temperature? I imagine it's quite consistent here in the conservatory."

"Yes, I've made sure of that. It's warm, just like their tropical home. Do you think it could use anything else?" A hint of vulnerability laced her voice, as if she valued his opinion. She looked up at him, eyes wide and expectant, and his chest tightened. Had anyone else ever looked at him like this, as if he were the most important thing in the world?

"Perhaps some organic compost or well-rotted manure mixed into the soil. That should provide the nutrients it needs," Nate suggested, though his thoughts were less on the orchid and more on the woman beside him. He couldn't help but notice the way she watched him, her gaze full of curiosity and something deeper, something that mirrored his own feelings. He forced his gaze back to the plant. "And look at those roots! Nice and green, neither too dry nor soggy."

Mary let out an exaggerated breath, her shoulders relaxing as she leaned a little more into him. Her arm pressed against his, warm and soft, and his breath hitched. "I'm relieved to hear that. I've read about their aerial roots needing proper ventilation."

"You're a natural at this. All your plants look very robust. Have you considered expanding your collection of rare plants?" Nate pulled her a little closer, his fingers brushing against hers, testing the boundaries. Her reaction, the soft gasp, the way her fingers tightened around his, holding on as if she didn't want to let go, it all rewarded him.

His heart hammered in his chest as he leaned in, feeling her lean into him in return. Her gaze lifted to his, wide and questioning, the desire burning within unmistakable.

"Oh, I've thought about it," she said, her voice breathy, her eyes locked on his. She hesitated for just a moment, then tilted her head, a silent invitation. "So many fascinating plants are available. But for now, I'm just enjoying watching this one flourish. I think I've taken over enough of Eleanor's home as it is. Poor thing, her painting area is now pushed to one draughty corner over there, while this gorgeous orchid is quite the focal point."

"I could spend hours here admiring your collection." *Admiring you*, he thought, though he kept that to himself. Warmth spread through his chest, filling him with a sense of rightness he hadn't felt in a long time.

"You're welcome to join me anytime, Nate. I'd love your company—and your expertise." Mary glanced at him through her lashes, her gaze filled with a soft invitation that sent his heart pounding.

Nate's heart skipped a beat. "Careful, Mary, I might accept your invitation. Nothing compares to tending plants with someone who shares the same enthusiasm. Besides, these orchids might grow even faster with a little friendly competition."

Mary laughed, the sound light, musical, and wrapping around him like a sweet embrace. "Competition, is it? Well, that might mean I have to visit your conservatory."

Her words seemed to hang in the air between them, laden with a meaning he couldn't miss. His breath hitched as he gazed down at her, the unspoken promise of what could be sparking between them like a live wire. He wanted to close the gap, to feel her lips on his, to make her his in every way that mattered.

"Challenge accepted." Nate grinned, the thought of having her in his home, in his space, stirring a possessive longing within him. "We can arrange a visit. But be warned, I have a few tricks up my sleeve."

"I look forward to seeing them." Mary nudged his arm, her touch lingering. "And perhaps we can exchange more than just gardening tips."

"I'd like that very much." Nate's gaze lingered on her, his desire for her growing stronger with each passing second. He leaned in and pressed a soft kiss to her lips. It was brief, but it sent a thrill through him, igniting a fire that had been smouldering within. Mary's eyes widened in surprise, but she didn't pull away.

Nate lowered his head, ready to kiss her again, when the sound of footsteps broke the spell. Nate stiffened as Emily, Mary's maid, bustled into the conservatory, her cheeks flushed, and a mischievous grin spreading across her face.

"Miss Mary, Lady Eleanor sent me to monitor you two. I'm to ensure no mischief is afoot."

Mary stepped back, putting some distance between them, and Nate felt the loss acutely. She didn't meet his eyes, but her cheeks flushed, and fingers trembled as she let go of his hand.

"Oh, Emily, we were just discussing orchids. Hardly the stuff of scandal." Mary's voice wavered, and she cleared her throat, trying to regain her composure.

"Orchids, eh?" Emily winked at Nate, clearly enjoying her role as chaperone far too much. "Well, I suppose if anyone could make plants exciting, it'd be you two. And don't worry, I'll make sure nothing untoward happens on my watch."

Nate forced a chuckle, trying to shake off the lingering desire that clung to him like a second skin. "Your diligence is much appreciated. We wouldn't want any orchid-related misadventures."

"Speak for yourself." Mary whispered, just loud enough for him to catch. Her playful glint dared him to try again, showing no embarrassment at almost being caught by Emily.

They lingered in the conservatory, but the magic of the moment had passed. When Mary announced they should return to the drawing room, he didn't resist. But his mind was already working on a plan— one that involved getting Mary to visit his home. Alone would be impossible, but a visit from the whole family would be tolerable if it meant he could steal a few precious moments with her.

As they walked back to the drawing room, Nate couldn't shake feeling her lips against his, the warmth of her touch still tingling on his skin. He was a man of action, sure of what he wanted. Mary stirred something deep within him, a desire he couldn't satisfy until he held her in his arms. If that meant navigating her family's watchful eyes and Emily's cheeky interference, so be it.

He glanced at Mary as they entered the drawing room, catching the small, secret smile she shot him when no one else was looking. It was a smile that promised more. More kisses, more shared moments, more of everything he craved.

For the first time in a long while, hope blossomed in his chest. Now all he had to do was persuade Mary to marry him sooner rather than later.

Chapter Fourteen

Mary paced in the library, twisting her fingers in the folds of her gown. She'd sought refuge there after both Eleanor and her mother chastised her for fidgeting in the drawing room. How could anyone expect her not to fidget? Heavens, what would have happened if Jane hadn't come into the conservatory when she did?

Nate would have kissed her a second time, perhaps just like he did after the fiasco at the Harrington's musicale, she was certain of it.

And if he had? Her heart raced at the thought. She wouldn't have just let him kiss her. She would have wrapped her arms around his neck, fingers tangling in his hair, desperate to keep him close. Oh, why did she indulge in so many romantic novels? What if Emily had found them in such an improper embrace? It didn't bear thinking about. No matter how much she longed to marry Nate, and she did, how could she hold her head high while society cut not just her but the Darrow family, for the scurrilous gossip spread by that cad Blackwood?

No. There was no choice but to wait until she cleared her name. Then Nate would propose, properly this time. She would gracefully accept, and all would be well.

She came to an abrupt halt in front of the fiction shelves, memories of Nate kneeling before her flooding back. Was it just three days ago? It felt like an eternity had passed. Was that his official proposal? What had he said? She rubbed her neck, trying to recall his exact words. It was more of a declaration, really. A statement that they would marry. And he promised to wait until her name was cleared, but then he'd qualified it by saying not for too long. What did he mean by that? Days, weeks, months? Was there a deadline she wasn't aware of?

A touch on her arm startled her, and she let out a small scream, grabbing a heavy novel to defend herself as she spun around.

"Goodness, Mary, you are as tightly wound as a clock spring. Whatever is the matter?" Olivia's soothing voice broke through her panic, and it was all the prompting Mary needed to collapse into her sister's arms, sobbing.

Olivia held her patiently, stroking circles on her back until the sobs dissolved into sniffles.

"You know very well what the matter is." Mary accepted the handkerchief Olivia offered and dabbed her cheeks dry.

"Let me rephrase the question. What has changed between now and the last time I saw you just before we dressed for dinner?"

Mary swallowed hard. "I don't want to wait to marry Nate, but how can I with this scandal hanging over my head?"

"We don't know the full details of the rumours—"

"No. But they must be dreadful for Lady Harington to ask us to leave." It took a concentrated effort to stop more tears from falling.

"Not necessarily. Some people are very cautious. At the hint of scandal, they act as though the victim of the rumours is contagious."

"I wish I knew. Then we could work out how to counter them..." Mary trailed off, catching the sound of Nate's rich baritone in the entrance hall.

"That's the spirit. Now wash your face before Nate notices you have been crying." Olivia gave Mary's arm a reassuring pat as she nudged her to the concealed servants' door.

Mary sprinted from the library and returned as Nate finished handing off his outerwear, her cheeks and lips pinched pink to draw attention away from her reddened eyes.

She crossed to him from the library door, every intention of dragging him aside for a serious conversation forgotten at the sight of him. She smiled. "Dearest Lord Everhart, it has been simply ages. I'm so glad to see the nettle rash has cleared up."

Nate lifted his brows as he took her hands in his. "As am I. Falling headfirst into the weeds is the most embarrassing thing I have done in—"

"A week?" she teased, finishing the sentence for him.

"How are you, my love?" he asked sweetly. "Has the prickly heat, ah, irritation subsided?"

She swatted his arm and lowered her voice. "Ladies do not suffer from prickly heat."

"What on earth are you two whispering about?" Lady Beatrice tapped her way towards them. "I'm sure dinner is about to be announced. Nate, do escort Mary to the table."

Nate winked at her and offered his arm. She took it, relishing the steady strength beneath the fine fabric of his coat. The others were already gathering in the dining room, and Nate guided her to two chairs side by side. As she sat, he subtly shifted her chair closer to his, close enough that the occasional brush of his hand against hers sent delightful shivers down her spine.

Alice was the last to arrive, and she hurried to take the seat next to Mary.

Mary reached for Alice's hand under the table and whispered, "Dearest, what is it?"

"I'll tell you later," Alice whispered back, the quiver in her voice unmistakable, her skin blotchy and eyes watering.

"Is hay fever troubling you again, my dear?" Eleanor, ever observant, asked. "Perhaps you would be more comfortable with a tray in your room?"

Alice nodded, her relief palpable. Eleanor summoned her own maid and ensured she accompanied Alice to her room before she signalled the start of the dinner service.

Lady Beatrice huffed but kept her own council. Mary couldn't blame her. Alice had never suffered from hay fever. Something was amiss, and she would get to the bottom of it later. If Lord Lynden was the cause, he would have to answer to her.

Mary started as a servant placed a bowl of soup before her. Nate's fingertips found hers on the table, and she stole a glance at him, her heart swelling with warmth. His presence at the family table felt natural, as if he belonged in her family as much as they belonged together. This was why her sisters looked sappy-eyed at their husbands so often. It was what she had been waiting for, what she needed, and now that she had it, she would never let it go.

If only Alice could find the same happiness. Another reason Mary needed to clear her name, and soon.

"Ah, white soup." Lady Beatrice's voice cut through Mary's thoughts. The older woman surveyed the table with her usual sharp gaze. "A favourite of mine. I hope the cook has prepared it with the proper amount of nutmeg."

Mary smiled to herself as Alex replied with a teasing grin, "I'm sure she has, Grandmother, as always. I must warn you, Lord Everhart, she's a harsh critic with soup."

Mary dipped her spoon into the creamy broth, its warmth spreading through her. She stifled a laugh, knowing Nate was watching her, waiting for her reaction. When their gazes met, she couldn't resist winking at him, a small gesture that felt intimate, secretive—just for the two of them.

Conversation flowed around the table, and Mary soaked in the comfort of it all—the laughter, the teasing, the sense of belonging. But it was Nate's presence that made it even more special. She felt his gaze on her, a constant, reassuring weight that anchored her in the present. When Caroline spoke up, her mischievous tone unmistakable, Mary braced herself.

"Lord Everhart," Caroline began with a smirk as the fish course was served, the delicate aroma of poached sole with shrimp sauce filling the room. "I've heard you're quite the expert in orchids. Tell us, do you speak to them as much as Mary does?" She lowered her voice as if whispering a secret. "She even sings to them occasionally."

Amused titters circled the table. Mary was used to her family's light-hearted jests about her hobby, but Nate wasn't. She nudged his foot under the table, a silent signal she was on his side.

"Only when they're unruly, Lady Caroline." Nate rubbed his chin as if contemplating his response further, his amusement not far below the surface. "It's remarkable what a stern word can do to coax a bloom into obedience. Though I must admit, I've found 'The Ash Grove' to be a soothing melody, perfect for serenading especially beautiful blooms."

Mary couldn't hold back her laughter, the sound bubbling up despite her best efforts.

Olivia raised her brow in amusement. "It seems our Mary has found someone who understands her passions."

"Indeed." Mary glanced at Nate with undisguised affection. "It's rare to find a man who appreciates both orchids and roast mutton."

"Ah, the genuine test of a gentleman," James added with a chuckle, raising his glass as the roasted mutton was served, accompanied by simple, comforting boiled potatoes and carrots in butter. "But the real question is—how does he handle stewed celery?"

The table erupted in laughter again, and Mary relaxed further, the last remnants of tension easing from her shoulders. She caught Nate's gaze again, and a silent exchange of warmth and gratitude passed between them.

The main course gave way to dessert, but Mary couldn't savour the light, frothy lemon syllabub. It was getting too close to after dinner. The time that Alexander had decreed would be their war council. Decisions had to be reached regarding the Blackwood threat to the family.

When Eleanor rose to lead the ladies into the drawing room, Mary began to follow, but she hesitated, gripping the back of her chair. "Do not be long, gentlemen. We have much to discuss."

Alexander turned to her, his expression stern. "We will not be joining you this evening, Mary." He gestured around the table, where only the men of the family now sat. "We have a great deal to discuss."

Mary folded her arms as her resolve hardened. "You expect to have this discussion without me, Lady Beatrice, Eleanor, and especially poor Alice? We are all impacted by this."

Alexander remained silent.

Nate stood and stepped toward her. "Mary, this could get ugly. It is no place for a lady."

Mary glowered back at them both. "Fine. Do as you wish. We will hold our own council, and do not expect to be included in whatever actions we decide to take." She swept from the room with head held high.

She flounced into the drawing room and flopped onto the middle of the sofa, still fuming. To her surprise, Eleanor, Lady Beatrice, Olivia, and her mother all followed her in.

Eleanor sat beside her and patted her knee. "I couldn't have said it better myself."

Her mother sat in the armchair before the fire. "Caroline will be along shortly. She is just seeing Charlotte to her room."

"And I have sent for Alice. No matter how many tears she has shed, she needs to be included." Lady Beatrice eased herself into the opposite armchair as Eleanor rang the bell for tea. She pointed at Mary. "Men always think they know best and expect us to believe the same. The floor is yours, my dear."

Mary swallowed, uncertain. The enormity of what the family faced almost overwhelmed her.

"Let us wait for Alice and tea." Eleanor gave Mary a playful smile. "Then Mary can take the floor like the Duke of Wellington guiding his valiant troops to triumph."

A ripple of laughter followed, even from Lady Beatrice. Mary cast Eleanor a grateful smile, though her nerves still danced. Perhaps, in the meantime, a divine spark of inspiration might strike. One could only hope.

Chapter Fifteen

It couldn't have been more than a few moments since the ladies made their dramatic exit, though it felt like minutes of shocked silence. Each second hammered at Nate's nerves.

Nate pushed back his chair, the scrape loud in the stillness. "I know about you two, but I'm not comfortable leaving our lovely ladies to their own devices."

"How much trouble can they get into?" James chuckled, though uncertainty crept into his voice.

"Have you met our wives?" Alexander stood, a grim smile tugging at his lips. "What was I thinking? The Darrow sisters alone are a force to be reckoned with. Add my grandmother and you have quads of diabolical cunning."

"Septets of infernal ingenuity, including Caroline and Alice." A prickle of concern tickled Nate's neck as he moved to the door. "Once they put their heads together..."

The three men almost collided in their haste to leave the room, Alexander pausing only to request port and Madeira in the drawing room.

Nate led the way. He didn't bother with knocking, just pushed the door open and strode inside, only to find all the women gathered, incongruously laughing. The tension in his shoulders eased, quickly replaced with a renewed sense of determination when the laughter ceased, and all seven women turned haughty glares upon them.

Lady Beatrice glanced at the watch she kept hanging on her belt. "At least it didn't take too long for you to come to your senses, gentlemen."

The tea service arrived, snapping the silent tension. The clinking of china and soft murmurs of the maids arranging the tray providing a brief distraction, but Nate still found himself hyper-aware of every sound. His gaze lingered on Mary's down-turned face as she pointedly refused to look at him. Had he hurt her by trying to protect her? By trying to exclude her from what couldn't be a calm discussion? The thought twisted his insides.

Alexander stood with ankles crossed, leaning on the mantle, his intent to take charge clear. Just as well, Nate focused only on Mary as he moved to sit beside her.

"I won't apologise for trying to protect you," Nate whispered, taking Mary's hand, and kissing her fingertips. "But I am sorry for trying to exclude you. You have every right to be part of this discussion."

She didn't respond, but she relaxed. It would have to do for now. Nate's heart ached to ease her worries, to shield her from the world's ugliness. But she wasn't a delicate flower to shelter—she was a sturdy oak, capable, and intelligent. He had to let her stand beside him, not behind.

James, ever practical, fetched a chair and sat beside Olivia. Alice looked much better, her jaw set and eyes full of fire.

"It is clear we must act together, united as one family, if we are to overcome these threats." Alexander raised his glass as if toasting to their unity.

Lady Beatrice, her expression as sharp as ever, accepted a cup of tea from Eleanor and nodded. "A wise decision."

Nate squeezed Mary's hand again, hoping she could feel the sincerity in his touch. He loved her, and he would do whatever it took to keep her safe.

"Perhaps I should start by summarising the challenges that face us." Alexander drained the liquid in his glass. The strain showed on his face, and Nate felt his pain. It couldn't be easy to share the precious secret that his grandmother had tried to guard. Not even with his closest friends and family.

Alexander gave a nervous cough, his voice filled with emotion, though it remained as steady as ever. "I must start with the documents that fell into Blackwood's hands quite by accident, which he has used to devastating effect. I'm guessing these documents led him to target the Weston family. It gave him a means to blackmail, and a way to pressure me to permit his marriage to either Mary or Caroline to gain access to the Weston family fortune and the wealth, prestige, as well as influence of the Duke of Wallingford. I can only presume he started spreading rumours about Mary to twist the screws further."

Nate's jaw clenched. The thought of Blackwood anywhere near Mary sent a surge of anger through him. "Or her rejection of him triggered a spiteful reaction."

Alexander conceded the point with a nod. "The issue is bigger than restoring Mary's reputation, as we once thought. Though he could still aim to ruin her reputation so much that she will have no choice but to accept his proposal, meaning he could keep his blackmail material and increase his demands for funds."

He paused, his gaze flicking to Alice. "Alice being followed suggests that we are all under scrutiny by someone hired by Blackwood or a reporter. Unfortunately, Blackwood's connection to Nate's brother, the duke, means his influence extends further than we believed, and his reach is long."

Nate's blood boiled at the mention of his brother. He kept his tone even though it took all his restraint. "I will deal with my brother."

Alexander lifted his palm in a calming gesture. "We will deal with him as part of the grand plan, Nate."

Nate nodded, though frustration gnawed at him.

Mary spoke up, "We cannot forget that Blackwood's machinations have affected Alice as well. Thanks to him, her promising courtship with Lord Lynden is at risk."

Alexander lifted his brow. "Courtship? The impudent imp has not approached me."

Alice cast a reproving glare toward Mary before responding, "Only because I begged him not to, Uncle Alexander, not yet. Please don't blame him."

Alexander sighed, lifting his palm again in a gesture of peace. "We will discuss your Lord Lynden later, I promise. In the meantime, I believe we have two key challenges. We must remove Blackwood's leverage and restore Mary's reputation so she will agree to wed Nate as soon as earthly possible."

Nate's heart swelled at the thought, though the weight of the situation tempered his joy.

Lady Beatrice's eyes narrowed, her expression hardening. "It will not be easy. Blackwood is cunning, and he won't keep those documents where anyone can find them."

"But we must," Eleanor interjected. "If we obtain them, we strip away his power. Without them, he has nothing. Mary's reputation will restore itself with her engagement to Nate. No need for her to be forced into marriage by that blackguard."

Nate tightened his grip on Mary's hand. The thought of losing her to Blackwood was intolerable.

A murmur of agreement spread through the room, heads nodding.

James leaned forward, elbows on his knees. "I know someone who might help—a man who specialises in retrieving...difficult items. It will be dangerous, but I believe it's our best chance."

Nate's protective instincts flared. "Can we trust him?" He didn't want to offend a duke, soon to be his brother-in-law, but the stakes were too high.

James nodded, unfazed. "Trustworthy and skilled at what he does. Very skilled."

"We must prepare for anything." Nate took a deep breath, quelling rising anxiety. "If Blackwood suspects us, he may move the documents or use them to force Mary's hand even sooner."

"We need a distraction." Eleanor stood and paced with a determined air. "Something to draw him away from his home long enough for us to retrieve the documents."

Olivia nudged James. "Isn't it time you introduced your new duchess to London Society?"

James frowned. "Aren't you well known enough, my love?"

"It's perfect." Eleanor hugged Olivia. "There is no way Blackwood will ignore an invitation from the Duke of Wallingford. He might even think his plan is working."

Eleanor resumed her pacing, her excitement now palpable. "We'll need to keep up appearances, make sure he stays at the ball and suspects nothing."

Hope surged in Nate's chest. This could work. But Mary stood, her hands on her hips. "You do not expect me to be nice to him?"

"Of course, my dear, and you will put on a marvellous act." Eleanor flashed her a confident smile.

Nate tugged Mary back to his side. "I won't be far away." No way he'd let her face this alone.

"We should invite Nate's brother too. Make sure he sees how united we are, and how much we love Nate." With an evil smirk, Eleanor rubbed her hands together.

Nate stood. "Now see here—"

"An excellent suggestion." Alexander stepped between them. "I won't let that man to besmirch my family without redress."

Nate knew better than to argue when Alexander was in this mood. His resolve was granite, immovable once set, and Nate had learned long ago that pushing against it was futile. He backed down, though every instinct in him bristled at the thought of his brother near Mary. He'd trust Alexander's judgement... for now.

He took his seat beside Mary again, and she squeezed her hand around his, her touch soothing the storm inside him.

"Never mind, dearest, I won't be far." She whispered the gentle tease, echoing his own earlier promise.

A smile tugged at his lips. The minx, using his own words to comfort him. It was a reminder of why he loved her so fiercely—her spirit, her wit, the way she knew what he needed to hear, even when he didn't.

"Excuse me. I have letters to write and send." James stood and kissed Olivia's cheek. "The editor at the Times is an acquaintance. I will see what I can do about their social column."

Eleanor, ever the planner, clasped Olivia's hands with a determined glint in her eyes. "We have a ball to plan."

"You know how much I love balls." Olivia let out a theatrical groan. "But at least this one is for a good cause."

Mary sighed. "What are Alice and I to do?"

"You'll be the star attractions of the ball," Eleanor declared with her usual confidence.

Olivia gave a slight cough, her broad smile betraying her amusement. "I believe I will be the star."

"Of course not. Everyone will use the excuse you have so generously provided, but truly, they will all want to see if the second youngest Darrow sister has grown a devil's tail."

"It's not that bad." Mary gestured.

Caroline, silent all evening, piped up. "I can go to the ball, can't I? I'm seventeen now. My friend, Poppy, has already curtsied to the Queen, and she is a few months younger than me."

The dowager countess responded, "You may attend for a short while, as you are family, but no later than eleven."

Caroline groaned but didn't argue.

"Nate." Alexander's voice pulled Nate from his thoughts. He gestured to the door. "We need to discuss logistics. Let's retire to my study."

Nate hesitated and turned to Mary. He took her hand again and brought it to his lips to place a soft kiss on the back of her fingertips. "We aren't excluding you, my love. It's important that you stay here and remind Eleanor that she must protect you. And I promise, no secrets."

Mary gave him a soft smile, one that sent warmth flooding through him. "No secrets. I promise the same."

Nate rose to follow Alexander from the room. At the door he cast one last glance at Mary, his heart clenching with the weight of what lay ahead. He blew her a kiss, unable to resist the slight gesture that made her giggle—an innocent sound that momentarily banished the shadows lingering in his mind.

But as he stepped into the dimly lit corridor, leaving behind the safety of her presence, the reality of their situation crashed back over him. Blackwood was out there, lurking, plotting, and every move they made flirted with danger. Nate's resolve solidified as he followed Alexander to the study. He would do whatever it took to protect Mary.

A single thought echoed in his mind, tightening his grip on the hilt of the resolve he carried like a sword—if Blackwood wanted a war, he would get one.

Chapter Sixteen

Crisp morning air laced with the delicate scent of blooming roses greeted Mary as she stepped down from Nate's carriage. The famed Kew Gardens stretched before her, a vast expanse of cultivated beauty, towering trees and vibrant flowerbeds dancing in the sunlight. Nate had declared today was for serenity and simple pleasures, a break from two days of ball planning for her and logistics planning for him.

How was it possible that even amidst such beauty, she couldn't quiet her mind? Perhaps because a web of deceit was ready to ensnare them.

Nate was at her side before her thoughts coalesced, his presence a steadying force. She shook her parasol open, and he offered his arm with a warm smile that made her heart skip—a smile she was relying on more than she'd ever thought possible. Lady Beatrice and Alice trailed behind them, Alice's energy almost bubbling over as she scanned the gardens with wide eyes.

She had been so eager to join her and Nate, even Lady Beatrice had eyed her suspiciously.

"Is it not the most glorious day, Mary?" Nate's voice carried a note of genuine wonder as he gestured to the surrounding greenery.

Mary agreed, her voice soft. She relaxed, and the garden's tranquil beauty seeped into her bones. She inhaled deeply, catching the fragrant mix of lavender and honeysuckle, and for a moment, all thoughts of rumours, scandal, ruined reputations, and forged documents fled from her mind. If only she could bottle this peace, she could carry it with her into the storms that awaited her.

"I thought you might enjoy it." Nate's tender gaze was enough to make her cheeks warm. He laughed. "Have I told you how much I love your blush? It's even prettier than the Maiden's Blush blooms we will find in this garden."

Mary huffed. "I don't think the mottled shade—the colour my cheeks are wont to turn—is as lovely as the famous, delicate, pale pink of the famous Rosa alba. Did you know it dates to medieval times, is one of the most popular blooms in English gardens, and loved for its delicate fragrance?"

"We will come across some soon enough." Nate guided Mary through an arch of climbing roses with his hand gently on her back. "Your knowledge of botany continues to amaze me."

"Now you are making fun of me." Mary slapped his arm. She met his gaze full on. He looked at her as if she were the only person in the world, as if every word she spoke mattered, as if he cared more for her than himself. She swallowed, conscious that they were very much in the public eye, though she always felt safe when Nate held her close. "Thank you for bringing me here."

Nate's smile widened, and they continued their stroll down the gravel path, Alice's footsteps and Lady Beatrice's cane pattering behind them.

"I believe I see someone I know," Alice said, her voice filled with bright enthusiasm. Mary turned and caught the mischievous glint in her cousin's eyes. Alice picked up the front of her skirt and darted toward a grinning man. Her plan was all too transparent, and before Mary could protest, Alice was already walking back with Lord Lynden.

Nate chuckled beside her. "She's made her escape. It appears we are on our own, my love."

Lady Beatrice tutted behind them. "What am I, young man? A ghost?"

"You, my lady, make the most accommodating chaperone in the history of—"

"Enough. I will sit on that bench under the ash tree. You two will stroll around the lake, within my sight always. Is that clear?" Lady Beatrice gestured to the bench she had in mind, her tone brooking no argument.

Nate took her arm and assisted her to the bench.

"Send those two reprobates over here, will you?" She tapped his leg with her walking cane.

She glowered at Alice and Lord Lynden, standing far too close and looking far too intimate for any public setting. Nate did as she asked, and once Alice and Lord Lynden joined them, Lady Beatrice repeated her instructions.

Nate offered his arm again, his smile just as warm, Mary's heart skipping as usual. A bright laugh escaped her before she could rein it in. A flicker of nervousness settled in her chest. Their engagement hadn't been announced. It wasn't proper to be alone with him like this, but then, propriety was a fragile thing, and she was growing weary of living in its shadow.

"If Blackwood should see us, will it spoil our plans?" she whispered to him.

Nate lowered his head to whisper back. Even gardens had ears, after all. "Not at all. Our engagement is a guarded secret. He has no reason to see me as anything other than a rival for your affection."

They walked in comfortable silence for a while. Mary savoured the moment, beautiful birdsong, a gentle breeze rustling leaves on the trees, filtered sun on her skin, the vibrant flowers, and most of all, the steady presence of Nate at her side. If only they could stay in this moment, this perfect, untroubled moment forever.

They came upon a courting bench nestled beneath a canopy of wisteria. The flowers hung in delicate clusters, their purple hue so vivid it seemed almost unreal. Nate led her to the bench, and they sat both apart and close together, the world narrowing to just the two of them.

Mary glanced around in awe. "I've never seen this park so full of blooms. It feels like a world apart from reality."

Nate nodded, his gaze thoughtful. "Here, surrounded by nature's beauty, it's easy to forget about one's troubles."

"And we have so many to forget." Mary's smile faltered. "If only we could stay here forever."

"We have both been so busy. Tell me how you are feeling."

Mary hesitated, her fingers twisting in her lap. Her entire life she'd been taught to avoid feelings, to push anything negative to the back of her mind. To especially talk to men without saying much. But she wanted to tell Nate everything. She wanted him to reassure her, to calm the gnawing anxiety that had been her constant companion since the rumours began.

Mary opened her mouth, but her voice faltered. She took a steadying breath, the scent of wisteria filling her senses, and tried again. "I'm worried, Nate. About my reputation, of course, but also about Alexander and his grandmother, and about us."

"You have nothing to worry about regarding us." Nate's expression softened, and he reached out, taking her hand in his. His touch was warm, reassuring. "Don't worry about those who speak ill of you, Mary. Their words hold no weight with those who matter."

"But they could ruin everything." Fear tinged her voice.

Nate squeezed her hand, his grip firm but comforting. "Mary, you are a lady in full bloom. Some people may try to bring you down, but your spirit is too strong, too vibrant, to be dimmed by petty gossip. There is nothing they can say or do that will change my regard for you."

Mary's heart swelled at the sincerity in his eyes. His words were like a balm, soothing deep-seated fears she hadn't realized had taken root. She no idea how he always knew what she needed to hear, but she would be forever grateful.

"As for our future, I promise you, we will face whatever comes together."

"I fear that somehow Blackwood will force Alexander's hand." Mary swallowed a hard lump in her throat. This was one fear she had not yet voiced aloud to anyone. Her breath hitched, and she blurted out the rest, "Force Alexander's hand! Force me to marry him."

"Mary." Nate lifted her chin with his fingertip. "I vow there is nothing on earth that will push Alexander to force you into such a union. And nothing on earth that will stop me from protecting you."

If passersby weren't glancing into their alcove every moment or so, Mary would have thrown herself into his lap and kissed him as senseless as his kisses left her. But as it was, she settled for showing him her emotion in the brightest smile she could muster.

They spoke of lighter things after that—of botany and the gardens they wished to visit. Nate shared his dream of cultivating a garden that would rival the very one they sat in, and Mary eagerly planned future excursions with him. It felt so natural, so right, as if their lives had always been entwined.

"Here they are." Alice's voice cut through Mary's reverie, and she glanced up to see Alice approaching with a huge grin on her face, towing Lord Lynden behind her. "I told you they would canoodle somewhere."

"Alice, we are aiming to keep a low profile," Nate gently rebuked. But he stood and shook Lynden's hand. "Perhaps we should collect Lady Beatrice and visit Gunter's, as it has become so warm.

The two men nudged the ladies in front of them, and Alice took Mary's arm in hers.

When the men had fallen far enough behind. Alice squeezed Mary's arm. "I'm so happy. I could die right here with no regrets."

"Has he—"

Alice shushed Mary. "Not exactly, but we have an understanding."

Mary's heart sank. "Does this understanding pertain to the circumstances—"

Alice shushed her. "He wishes to wait until after you wed Nate, but he has promised me, and that is good enough. For you will marry, and soon. Then the ton will forget all the gossip that cad Blackwood has spread, and then delight in your happiness."

Alice's happiness was contagious. But how could she be so certain? The ever-present weight of worry rarely left Mary's stomach. "You are very optimistic."

"I am. And you should be too."

Optimism felt like a luxury Mary couldn't afford. Not yet.

They arrived where Lady Beatrice waited for them and paused a moment for the men to catch up. Mary was about to take Nate's arm when a group of young ladies approached. One of them, a sharp-featured debutante Mary recognised as one of those who treated her like a leper at the musicale, sidled up to Nate.

"Lord Everhart." She was purring, her tone laced with false sweetness. "How delightful to see you here. Though I must say, I am surprised to see you in the company of... certain people." She flicked a glance at Mary, a haughty curl in her lip.

Mary stiffened, the insinuation clear. The insult, veiled as it was, stung like a wasp. Her anger bubbled up, but before she could respond, Nate's expression hardened.

"Miss Abernathy." His voice was colder than Mary had ever heard it. "I see you are well-versed in the art of insinuation. However, I must correct you. Lady Mary Darrow is a woman of grace and honour, and I would advise you to not spread falsehoods."

Miss Abernathy blinked, taken aback by the forcefulness of his words. "I... I only meant—"

"I believe you've said enough," Nate interrupted, his tone leaving no room for argument. "Now, if you'll excuse us."

Without another word, he took Mary's arm and led her away, leaving Miss Abernathy to stand there, speechless. Mary's pulse pounded in her ears. Old Mary would have walked away like a dormouse. New Mary had felt like giving the woman a dressing down, though she didn't know how. But New Mary had also never seen Nathaniel so fierce, so protective, and so very handsome.

As they walked away from the confrontation, Nathaniel's grip on her arm softened. "Are you alright?"

She nodded, calmer now, though the remnants of the encounter still prickled beneath her skin. "Yes, thank you. I don't know what I would have done without you."

"I'm sure you would have handled her with your usual aplomb. But you don't have to face these things alone." Nate filled his voice with an intensity that made her breath catch. "I will always stand by your side, Mary. Always."

The words hung between them, charged with unspoken emotions. Mary's pulse quickened, her heart swelling with the love she felt for this man. She felt it in the way he looked at her, the way his touch lingered on her skin, and in the way the world seemed to pause around them, as if waiting for something to happen.

Before she could respond, a figure caught her eye—a man with a notepad, hovering almost within a copse of trees, watching them with far too much interest. Mary's stomach twisted. It had to be a reporter. She pointed the man out to Nate, and he took off after him.

He returned not long after. "Lost him in the shrubbery, damn it. Excuse me, ladies."

Alice lifted her hands to her mouth. "What if he writes about us?"

Nate followed her gaze, his expression darkening. But when he turned back to her, his eyes were the calmest blue hues. "Let him write what he will. We will face whatever comes, as a family, together."

The reassurance in his voice, the absolute certainty, eased some of the fear gnawing at Mary.

But Alice still wrung her hands. "Archie, your family will see—"

He shushed her with his finger on her lips. "I agree with Lord Everhart. Let him write, let them publish what they will. I will not turn away from you again, dearest."

Alice looked as if she were ready to melt into a puddle, and Mary couldn't help a fond smile.

Nate shrugged. "We are cavorting in public. Let's get the largest ice cream Gunter's has." He lowered his voice. "We will celebrate secret engagements."

"Here, here," Lord Lynden agreed.

Nate took Lady Beatrice's arm and helped her back to the waiting carriage.

"Secret engagements?" Lady Beatrice settled herself in the carriage and arched her brow. "How very modern of you. Next, you will be telling me you plan to announce it in the society pages right after that reporter documents your escapades."

Nate chuckled. "Let's not add to the scandal sheets."

"Pity," Lady Beatrice replied, her tone amused. "I do so enjoy reading about the antics of the younger generation. They provide endless fodder for my disdain." She looked at Alice and Lord Lynden, then back at Mary and Nate. "But I suppose, if you must be scandalous, you might as well do it with style." She gave Mary a wink as she settled back into the leather.

As she let Nate hand her into the carriage, Mary felt something shift inside her. Nate was more than just a suitor, he was a partner, a protector. Someone she could trust with not just her future, but her heart.

And for the first time in a long while, hope blossomed.

Chapter Seventeen

The day of the Duchess of Wallingford's ball started with brilliant sunshine, but it seemed no amount of golden light could chase away the shadow of dread curling inside Mary's chest.

She sat beside Alice at the breakfast table, the air heavy with the scent of roses that normally soothed her soul. Not today. Today the sweet scent, overlaying what was left of breakfast, felt cloying, almost suffocating. The delicate China teacup in Mary's hand trembled slightly as she watched Alice furiously scanning the latest edition of the Times, her expression darkening with every word she read.

"I cannot believe it, Mary. That reporter has indeed written about us!" Alice's whisper quivered with irritation as she thrust the newspaper toward Mary.

Mary's stomach knotted tighter. How could everything go so wrong? Unfortunately, her mother, Lady Beatrice and her sisters all stopped their chatter as she took the newspaper. Her heart sank further, as if she were being pulled into icy waters.

"Out with it, child. What scandalous headline have you inspired this time?" The gentleness of her expression softened Lady Beatrice's harsh words.

Mary forced a brittle smile and started reading. *"A Scandalous Interlude in the Gardens.* At least my name isn't in the headline." Mary's attempt at light-heartedness fell flat, so she cleared her throat and carried on reading snippets from the rather long article.

"Kew Gardens, typically a haven of tranquillity, was the unlikely setting for a rather dramatic exchange earlier this week, involving none other than Lord Everhart and Lady Mary Darrow, who has recently found herself at the centre of much speculation."

Mary let a deep sigh rumble from her mouth. The words blurred together. Gossip might only be words, but sharp edges were enough to cut through her composure. Why did everything come back to this speculation about her virtue? Couldn't anyone but her family and dearest Nate see her for who she really was? She forced herself to keep going.

"Miss Abernathy, with a tone described by onlookers as "honeyed but sharp," expressed her surprise at seeing Lord Everhart in what she insinuated to be less-than-desirable company. Her remark, veiled though it was, clearly aimed at Lady Mary, was met not with the expected embarrassment or quiet dismissal, but with a response as cold as it was swift.

"Lord Everhart, displaying a side of himself rarely seen in public, firmly rebuked Miss Abernathy, leaving the young lady visibly shaken."

"Your gallant knight, Mary. How very romantic." Caroline's dreamy sigh pulled Mary from her spiralling thoughts. The romanticism in her sister's voice almost made her laugh aloud. It was that or cry.

Lady Beatrice helped herself to another piece of toast. "It was a treat to see that spoilt young woman set down with a well-deserved rebuke. Though I know Mary could defend herself admirably."

"By seizing her in a headlock and thrusting her face into a nettle patch." Caroline giggled.

"What mischief did you girls involve yourself in as youngsters?" Lady Beatrice tutted.

Mary smiled faintly, a ghost of the joy she might have felt any other morning. No one answered Lady Beatrice, and fortunately she didn't push, because truth be told, the girls had run a little wild while their parents were wrapped up in themselves. It was only when Eleanor's redoubtable governess arrived, they had no choice but to rein in their behaviour.

Mary let out a sigh. The thought of Nate's defence still warmed her heart, but it shouldn't have been necessary. Lydia Abernathy was a cat who deserved no cream. She'd claw her way back to society sweetheart no matter who she had to shred. "Shall I read on?"

A chorus of yesses sounded, so Mary continued,

"It is rare that a gentleman of Lord Everhart's standing publicly defends a lady's honour in such a manner. Witnesses reported that the other young ladies present fell silent as Lord Everhart took Lady Mary's arm and led her away, his protective manner unmistakable.

"This bold defence by Lord Everhart, combined with his undeniable closeness to Lady Mary, is sure to fuel the already rampant speculation about their relationship. Will this public display of loyalty mark the end of the gossip that has plagued Lady Mary, or will it only add to the flames of rumour?

"We wait with bated breath to see what the next chapter in this unfolding drama will bring."

Mary set the paper down with trembling hands. "It's been three days. I hoped the reporter had forgotten all about it, but no, he had to publish, and on the very day of Olivia's ball, no less." Mary sighed again, the sound heavy with dread. "This could not have come at a worse time."

Alice, normally so full of confidence, nodded as she bit her lip anxiously. "And to think we tried so hard to avoid attention at Kew Gardens. All our efforts were in vain."

"Nonsense." Eleanor patted Mary's hand. "Blackwood is likely seething that you and Nate are growing closer. He will certainly show up at the ball. And James' contact will perform his *special task* and get us out of this bind."

"You are so optimistic, Eleanor. I wish I shared your confidence, but..." Mary couldn't finish. Though she didn't need to, everyone knew the risk. And no matter how much Mary loved Nate, how could she let Alexander and Eleanor lose everything just because she refused to marry Blackwood?

Eleanor hugged her tightly, her embrace full of strength. "No fretting, dearest. Alexander won't allow that man dictate who you wed. Now, didn't you and Alice promise to help Olivia with final preparations?"

"We did." Alice took Mary's hand and pulled her to her feet. "Come along, Miss Scandalous. Let's dress and spend a few hours with Olivia and her gorgeous babies."

Mary allowed Alice to lead her away, her cousin's constant chatter a blessing as she didn't need to contribute to the conversation at all. Her thoughts remained heavy, a tangle of doubt and fear. How she wanted to believe Eleanor's assurances. But if Blackwood held the evidence to blackmail them, shadows of uncertainty loomed too large to ignore.

The ballroom, when they finally entered late that evening, was a dazzling spectacle. London's elite already filled the space, the atmosphere alive with their conversation and laughter. Crystal chandeliers cast shimmering light across the elegant crowd. Everything was exactly as it should be, except for the tight knot in her stomach that refused to unravel.

As planned, Mary and Nate were amongst the last to arrive. She entered on Nate's arm, acutely aware of gazes following their every move —some curious, others judgmental, some feigning indifference, their backs turned, and their snooty noses in the air. A few were openly hostile, the weight of their gazes making her skin prickle with unease.

The Duke and Duchess of Wallingford greeted them warmly. The duke offered a nod of encouragement. "I'm glad you're here, Lady Mary. Let's show them what true nobility looks like."

Mary straightened, drawing strength from the loyal support of her sister and the duke. She would face the night with grace, no matter what challenges awaited.

Olivia pulled her to the side, her brow furrowed with concern. "Are you really alright? You seemed distracted earlier today. I promise we'll resolve everything. Blackwood arrived about thirty minutes ago, and James dispatched his man straight away."

Mary gripped her sister's hands. "I'm terribly afraid, Olivia, but I will be fine once this is over. More than fine." She tried to infuse her voice with all the optimism and confidence she wished she felt. The jittery pace of her words betrayed her though, and Olivia's wince implied Mary hadn't convinced her.

It was a good thing she didn't need to talk with any of the guests. No one was speaking to her, anyway. She could just hold her head high and pretend.

The names of her family filled her dance card—also planned. Blackwood would have to push one of her brothers-in-law or Nate to one side to get to her. At Eleanor's recommendation, she had pencilled in Nate's name for every waltz.

Each time the music swelled around them, she found solace in his arms twirling her around the dance floor. For a few precious moments, the world faded away. They moved together as if in a dream, the rhythm of the dance connecting them at a deeper level than she had imagined possible.

Nate leaned in, his voice a gentle murmur in her ear. "Whatever happens tonight, remember that I'm by your side. This night is just one of many we'll face together."

Mary's heart swelled with emotion as she nodded, her gaze meeting his. "I know, Nate. With you, I feel as if I can face anything."

"Next time around, I will slow down. The man standing next to the grandfather clock is the Duke of Haversham."

"Your older brother, Charles?" Mary twisted to get a good look at the man Nate had fought with over her.

Nate leaned in closer, his voice dropping to a low, conspiratorial whisper. "Steer clear of the man." His loving gaze softened the sharp edge to his words. "He's outdone himself this evening, clearly determined to remind everyone of his impeccable taste—if not his impeccable judgment."

Mary's curiosity piqued. "Oh? And how has he outdone himself?"

Nate smirked, his tone dripping with mock seriousness. "Well, for starters, he's wearing a coat so black it might as well be mourning for his lost integrity, assuming he had any to begin with. And his waistcoat? It's a shade of green so dark, I half expect him to disappear into the shadows, emerging only to strike some nefarious bargain with Blackwood."

Mary laughed softly, the image of Charles skulking around the ballroom amusing her despite the underlying tension. "And what about his cravat?" she asked, playing along.

Nate's grin widened, though it didn't reach his eyes. "Ah, the cravat. It's tied in such a convoluted knot, I'm convinced it's a symbol of his moral compass—completely twisted and impossible to unravel. To top it off, the Haversham family crest is emblazoned on his waistcoat in gold thread, as if to say, 'I am the duke, and my friendship with Blackwood makes us both untouchable.'"

Mary's smile faltered slightly at the mention of Blackwood, but Nate's teasing tone drew her back. She lifted her brow in mock disbelief. "So, you're advising me to stay out of his way?"

Nate replied with a chuckle. "Unless he's had a personality transplant, he's here to intimidate, to show everyone that the Haversham name stands above reproach. But you and I both know the truth." He paused, his voice softening slightly. "Just be careful, Mary. He's not just here for the fashion, he's here for the games."

Mary's heart fluttered at the intensity in Nate's gaze. "I suppose I'll have to avoid his path then, lest I get caught up in his schemes—or blinded by his sartorial brilliance."

Nate's smile returned, a little less guarded this time. "Exactly. But don't worry, I'll be right beside you, ready to cut through whatever web he and Blackwood try to spin."

Mary nodded, but she couldn't shake an unsettling feeling that grew within her. Blackwood lurked at the edge of the room, his dark eyes fixed on them with an intensity that sent a shiver down her spine. She refused to let it ruin the moment, but the weight of his gaze lingered. He had not yet made a move, nor had James announced success. Blackwood's presence was a constant reminder of the danger hanging over her head.

After dancing for what felt like hours, Mary excused herself, needing relief from the heat and a moment to collect herself. A small balcony was visible to the men who watched over her like hawks, so she knew she would be safe there for a moment.

The cool night breeze was a welcome relief, and she closed her eyes, letting it wash over her. Her solace was short-lived. A loud crash sounded from the front of the house, shattering the peaceful moment and garnering everyone's attention.

Except Blackwood.

He approached her with a sincere smile that made her blood run colder than if he'd openly snarled at her. He clutched her arm, his fingers digging into her skin. "Lady Mary, we must speak. A word in private?"

She tried to shout but nothing came out of her mouth. Panic constricted her throat as he pulled her through a side door she hadn't even noticed and into a dimly lit hallway. It had to be a service hall, but they were totally alone. Panic rose in Mary's chest as terror flooded through her veins, freezing her in place, like one of the gothic heroines she loved to read about.

Blackwood didn't stop until they reached what had to be the duke's study. The room was almost dark, lit only by the faint glow of a single candle in the bookshelf. He snicked the door shut behind them, trapping her inside with him.

Her mind screamed at her to run, to fight, to do something, but her body refused to cooperate. All she could do was watch in horror as Blackwood swept the contents of the desk onto the floor with one aggressive motion.

"I'm sure you understand the situation, my dear." He looked almost apologetic, his tone as smooth as when he invited her to the theatre weeks ago. "If word spreads that we were alone together, what's left of your reputation will be utterly ruined. Unless, of course, you agree to my terms."

The implications of his words crashed down on her, and with them came a wave of fury. He intended to either force himself on her or create the appearance that he had. The thought was enough to snap her out of her shock. Fear twisted into anger, hot and sharp, burning through the icy terror that had gripped her.

With a surge of defiance, Mary slapped Blackwood across the face, her hand stinging from the impact. But he only laughed, his grip on her wrist unrelenting. "You're a feisty one, aren't you?"

"Feisty?" Mary's voice trembled with a controlled fury, her eyes narrowing. "I am far beyond that, Lord Blackwood. You overestimate your power and underestimate my resolve."

"Come now. You have brought this upon yourself. I was perfectly willing to court you as a gentleman, but you can't seem to get your head around the reality of the situation."

"I know all about your blackmail, and Alexander won't stand for it." She tried to yank her wrist free, but his grip tightened.

"Do you truly believe that Alexander will permit his noble family name to be tarnished? He risks losing everything. Now, that doesn't help me. I need him well endowed with funds—"

"So you can blackmail him more, even if you had me?"

"Of course," Blackwood sneered, his eyes glinting with greed. "You are my insurance policy. Your dowry, while impressive, will not be enough to restore my estate. For that I need your well-placed, influential, and wealthy relatives. Take a seat, my dear, your options will narrow very, very soon."

He tried to nudge her to the sofa, but Mary dug in her heels and refused to sit. If she somehow escaped his grasp, she had to reach the door before he did.

Fear coiled around her, tightening its grip. Suddenly, the door burst open. Relief flooded her senses—Nate was rescuing her.

But when she saw who stood in the doorway, her hope dwindled.

Nate's brother, the Duke of Haversham, swept into the room, his face a mask of exaggerated shock. Mary quickly saw through the façade. The man couldn't act to save his life.

"What is going on here?" His voice boomed unnaturally loud, clearly designed to draw attention. Within moments, the doorway filled with onlookers, eyes widening and whispers growing louder as the scandalous scene unfolded before them.

Panic twisted in Mary's chest. This was exactly what she had feared. This time there would be no escaping with the claim that everything was just Blackwood's lies. This time, she had been caught alone, behind closed doors, with a man who was not her kin.

She searched desperately for a way out, but the walls seemed to close in. How on earth would she get out of this unscathed, with her reputation intact and her future not in tatters? The answer eluded her, and dread settled in its place. Maybe her silence was just making things worse, but if she tried to defend herself, society would label her a harridan of the worst kind.

One thing was certain—whatever happened next would change everything.

Chapter Eighteen

A crowd had gathered before the open door to Wallingford's study. People pushed and shoved to get a better look at whatever was going on. Nate pushed his way to the front, his heart hammering in his tightening chest. He'd turned away when the statue fell and smashed in the foyer.

Now Mary was missing, and so were Blackwood and his brother. He wasn't naïve enough to think the two weren't connected.

His breath hitched. If they harmed her, his brother's face would meet his fist.

Whispers took on a menacing edge, silks and satins rustled, the scent of perfume mingled with body odour and hair powder, but he barely registered any of it. He had to find her. Nothing else mattered.

Two rows of people stood between him and the doorway when he heard her voice, sharp, and laced with fear.

"How dare you insinuate I cobbled together a story to trap you in this room, then arranged for us to be found, forcing your hand in marriage."

"We have caught you red-handed, girl." The Duke of Haversham's pompous, disdainful voice travelled across the large foyer. "One of the

Darrow chits, aren't you? Typical. Trying to score another title like your sisters, I suppose."

Nate's vision blurred with anger. His brother's voice was like a vise tightening around his heart, but it was the sound of Blackwood's oily tones followed by a grunt that sent Nate into a near frenzy.

"If you do not unhand me, you cad." Mary's voice filled with a fiery determination that made Nate's heart swell with pride even as the back of his neck prickled with fear for her. "I will have no choice but to cause you harm."

Both Blackwood and his brother laughed.

Blackwood gave a sinister-sounding cough. "You've caught me and now you've changed your mind, is that it?"

"I decided some time ago, and my fiancé will have something to say to you, I am sure. You also, Your Grace." Mary practically spat out the last sentence.

But she was frightened, and every second he wasn't there to protect her felt like an eternity. Nate wanted to cheer her on, lift her out of harm's way, and break both Blackwood and his brother's faces, all at the same time. He couldn't do any of it from where he was, so he started shoving people out of his way with little regard for propriety. To hell with the shocked gasps and indignant murmurs. Nothing would stop him from reaching Mary.

He burst through the doorway, and his breath caught in his throat. The study was dim, flickering light from a single candle casting long shadows across the room. But the scene before him was clear.

Mary stood as far from Blackwood as she could. Even though he gripped her wrist in a punishing hold, she held a heavy ceramic weight in her free hand. The cleared desk, the overturned chair, and the malevolent gleam in Blackwood's eyes painted a picture that made Nate's blood boil. He was almost vibrating with anger, eyes blazing with fury when he saw Mary's distress.

"What in God's name is going on here?" His voice was a low growl, filled with barely contained rage as his fists clenched at his sides. "Unhand my fiancé right now."

Mary didn't hesitate. She dropped the weight onto Blackwood's foot. It hit its target before thudding against the floor. Blackwood grunted in pain, and she yanked her wrist free of his grip. She rushed to Nate, and he swung her into his arms, her composure cracking as she clung to him. "He... he tried to..."

"Fiancé? Heh." The Duke of Haversham twisted one of his cufflinks as he slid a disdainful gaze over Nate. "I do not recall giving approval for any engagement."

Nate ignored his pig-headed brother to make sure Mary was comfortable. Only then did he narrow his eyes and meet his brother's stony stare with one of his own. "I didn't ask."

"I will not permit you to tie yourself to this vile creature." Haversham flicked his hand in a dismissive gesture toward Mary, as if she were nothing more than a nuisance to be swept out with the rubbish.

He would also be tarnished by scandal by the end of the evening, but Nate didn't care. His brother had crossed a line. There was no coming back from this. Haversham wouldn't ask for forgiveness, and Nate sure as hell wouldn't offer. "We have had this discussion, brother dearest. I care not for your opinion, your title, or your money. I love Mary, and we will wed."

The crowd gathered in the doorway gasped as if in collective shock.

Mary clutched at his lapels. "He forced me into this room. He wouldn't let me out—"

Haversham interrupted her. "We have already heard Lord Blackwood's account. No one is interested in your lies and protestations—"

Nate snapped. He wasn't about to listen to another word. Without a second thought, he swung his fist. The force of the blow sent his brother stumbling back, his mouth split and bleeding. The sharp pain in Nate's knuckles was nothing compared to the satisfaction of silencing Haversham's pompous tirade.

Blackwood's smirk dropped into a scowl.

"You will pay for this, Blackwood." Nate's wrath was palpable as he rounded on the man. "You have overstepped all bounds of propriety for the last time."

Before either man could escalate the confrontation further, the Duke of Wallingford entered the room, his authoritative presence commanding. He took in the scene with a cold, calculating gaze. "It's clear what you intended to do, Blackwood. This will not go unchallenged."

Alexander followed, his posture imposing as he stepped into him the now crowded study. "There's no need for any further unpleasantness." He locked his gaze on each man. "Blackwood no longer has any hold over our family."

Mary gasped. "Is it true? It's over?"

Nate kissed the top of her head. "Yes, my love."

Alexander lifted his head, turned to address the crowd, and raised his voice. "You've all witnessed what happened here tonight. Blackwood has attempted to force my hand with blackmail and a vile attempt to tarnish Lady Mary's honour. This evening was always meant to be special. I'm announcing the engagement of my niece, Lady Alice, to Lord Lynden, and of my sister-in-law, Lady Mary, to Lord Everhart. I had rather hoped the circumstances were more celebratory than this."

The announcement sent a ripple of shock through the now sizable crowd, their excited murmurs filling the air like a swarm of buzzing bees.

Blackwood's face contorted with rage. "You don't know what you've done, Weston."

"Oh, but I do." Alexander turned his back to the crowd, his voice quiet yet deadly in its certainty. "You see, we found the originals in your safe, a copy under your mattress, and another copy with your lawyer. Even if you have more copies, I don't care. Only the originals matter, and you do not have them."

Blackwood stumbled back a step, colour draining from his face. "I still have a pretty story to tell—"

"Do it. I'd love a reason to share just how badly your estate is failing, how much debt you are hiding, and lay bare every misdeed you have ever done. So sad to see such a proud house fall so low. No doubt this led you to lies and despair. At least, that is what your lawyer will claim."

"How dare you—"

"Get out Blackwood." James stepped forward, his arms folded across his chest. "I will see that you are never welcome in society again."

Four burly footmen arrived and manhandled Blackwood from the study. He protested all the way to the front door, but it was too late. His fate was sealed. The Duke of Haversham, handkerchief clutched to his nose, tried to follow, but Nate pulled him back.

He cradled his arm around Mary. "Anyone who dares challenge her honour will answer to me."

His brother gave him a curt nod before leaving the house.

James called Nate and Mary into the foyer, and ball guests quickly surrounded them in all their finery. Nate's pulse had yet to settle, and though the crisis had passed, the air remained thick with unspoken judgement. As they stepped forward, Alexander came to stand alongside them, as did Lord Lynden, a silent show of support. The four men—related, thanks to the Darrow sisters—stood united, shoulder to shoulder, filling Nate with gratitude he'd carry to his dying day.

No matter what had happened in the cursed study, his family—his new family—stood together. The ton would not dismiss such a front.

Mary still clung to Nate's jacket, her fingers trembling. Her distress stirred something primal in him. Every instinct screamed to whisk her away, to gather her into his arms and shield her from eyes that still watched, eager for more scandal. He longed to kiss her senseless, to banish the fear from her eyes. But to do so here, in front of a throng of scrutinising stares, would be reckless.

Instead, with a tenderness that belied the storm within him, he kissed the back of her hand. The simple gesture held more meaning than any words he could utter. It was a promise, unspoken but understood, he knew. He was hers, and nothing—no slander, no scandal—would change that.

"Mary," he whispered against her ear. "Stand tall, my love. You are not alone."

She met his gaze and loosened her grip on his jacket. He helped her to stand tall and face the crowd. Though her slender frame still trembled, she lifted her chin, and Nate could not have been prouder. Even in this most vulnerable state, her strength shone through.

James stepped forward. "This engagement has my full support." His voice carried across the room with the authority befitting his title and standing. "Let this night celebrate their future, not a dwell on the past misdeeds of a once noble house."

Shock and whispers gave way to hesitant acceptance. A ripple of polite applause rose from those who feared offending the duke more than they wanted to gossip.

The ball resumed, though with a distinct energy. Nate accepted polite congratulations from several people, heartfelt well wishes from a smaller number. Mary, beside him, was far less composed. She mumbled her thanks, her eyes glazed and distant. She was holding herself together by sheer will alone, but the evening had taken an obvious toll. He had to get her away, let her process and recover separate from the judgemental scrutiny of the ton. Her hand brushed against his. The subtle tremor he felt solidified his decision. She had given more than enough of herself to the court of public opinion tonight.

With one last nod to those around him, Nate slipped his hand into Mary's and leaned closer. "We're leaving. You need rest, and I need to get you far from this place."

Mary's gaze flickered, and she gave him a fleeting smile before lowering her gaze again. He sent Alexander to organise his carriage, and guided Mary to one of the small balconies dotting the ballroom.

At a curt nod from Nate, the lone occupant scurried away, leaving Nate and Mary alone on the balcony. The cool night air was a balm to the tension of the evening, the twinkling stars like distant promises of peace.

Nate shrugged out of his jacket and wrapped it around Mary's shoulders.

She leaned into his chest. "Now we are engaged, we can have stolen moments together."

"We can, though not for long, or the harpies will gossip again." He took Mary's hands in his. "I meant what I said, Mary. We'll face whatever comes together. You're my future, and I'll protect that future with everything I have."

Tears prickled Mary's eyes, but her upturned lips told him they were tears of relief. "Are you sure? Are you not thinking me just too much trouble by now?"

Nate leaned in, pressing a gentle kiss to her forehead. "You are trouble. But you are my trouble. Besides, with Blackwood licking his wounds, and no doubt the new target of the gossip columnists, the scandal surrounding you will die down, and you will become the new darling of the social set."

"I believe I could live on a deserted island for a little while. Anywhere I could avoid all the social set. Except you, of course. In fact, how do you feel about eloping?"

Nate chuckled. "Eleanor would never forgive you, which means Alexander would never forgive me. This is just the beginning, my love. We'll have our happily ever after, no matter what. But I'm glad you mentioned eloping."

Mary lifted her brow at him, her mouth opened in shock.

Before she could question him further, Nate closed the distance between them. He captured her lips in a deep, tender kiss that stole his breath and sent his heart soaring.

Epilogue

FOUR MONTHS LATER

The Caribbean Sea stretched out before Mary, an endless expanse of deep turquoise and shimmering sapphire gently lapping at the ship's hull. She stood at the edge of the deck, mesmerised. A warm breeze danced through her hair, teasing loose tendrils from her elegant bonnet. The air was thick with the scent of salt and sun-kissed wood, mingling with the exotic fragrance of the tropical flowers Nate had brought aboard the day before.

Mary gazed up at a vast dome of clearest blue sky, unmarred by even a single cloud. The sun hung high, casting a golden glow over everything it touched. She closed her eyes for a moment, letting the warmth seep into her skin, the gentle sway of the ship beneath her feet lulling her into a deep sense of peace.

Eleanor had talked her into a grand society wedding to show their family strength. In the end, Mary gave in, as it was easier than fighting against it. It had taken several torrid weeks to organise the wedding and plan the move into Nate's home, but their honeymoon in Greece was filled with blissful moments spent alone in a mansion by the sea.

This trip to explore native flora in the Caribbean Islands was Nate's

Christmas gift to her, the best gift she had ever received. After weeks at sea, a short stop in the Canary Islands, and more weeks at sea, they had finally arrived at their destination – over seven hundred islands, most tiny and uninhabited, but all holding potential for exciting discoveries. She couldn't wait to explore every single one!

When she opened her eyes again, her breath caught in her throat. A small island appeared on the horizon, lush and green, with palm trees spilling right down to the edge of pristine white sands.

A thrill of anticipation coursed through her. Nate had told her stories of the rare and exotic plants that grew in these remote places, plants that had never been documented in England. The thought of exploring such a place with Nate by her side filled her with excitement.

As if summoned by her thoughts, Nate appeared at her side, his presence as steadying and comforting as always. She turned to look at him, and her heart fluttered at the sight. He was dressed simply in a billowing white linen shirt, with tan breeches hugging his muscular legs. His wind-tousled hair added to the air of relaxed confidence that always seemed to surround him. But it was his eyes, deep and warm as the sea itself, that held her captive.

He smiled at her, a smile that made her feel as though the sun had just risen all over again. "It's breathtaking, isn't it?" His voice, a low, soothing rumble, sent a shiver down her spine.

Mary nodded, unable to tear her gaze away from the island ahead. "It's so different from the port we stopped in yesterday. I've never seen anything like it."

Nate smiled, his gaze intense as he took her hand. "I've never seen anyone as beautiful as you."

Her cheeks heated as a surge of warmth spread through her body. She didn't know how to respond, so she said the first thing that came to mind. "Do you think we will find hibiscus? I cannot believe the size of the blooms, so different from our flowers at home. Perhaps we will find more bougainvillea or frangipani, I've never smelled anything so intoxicating, or that purple orchid you pointed out to me."

She stopped to take a breath, and Nate laughed as he touched his fingertip to her lips. "I'm sure we will find all the treasures our hearts desire, my love. And we will bring them back home to remember this moment forever."

He spoke quietly to the captain before leading her to the front of the ship to better take in the breathtaking view. "This is a place where time stands still." Nate wrapped his arm around her waist. "A place where we can be ourselves."

"I've discovered I never want to wear gloves again." Mary turned to him, her heart overflowing with love and gratitude. "You've given me so much, Nate. More than I ever thought possible. How can I ever thank you?"

He looked down at her, his gaze intense and full of emotion. "You already have, Mary. Just by being here with me. As brave as any explorer, more beautiful than any bloom, with you, I feel complete. He cupped her face in his hands. "You are my treasure, my love."

Nate tightened his hand around hers, the already hard length of him pressing against her thigh as he pulled her closer. The warmth of his body seeped into hers, and a familiar fluttering started in her stomach, a sensation that had become so deliciously familiar since they had wed. His gaze dropped to her lips, and Mary's breath caught in her throat as she saw her own desire simmering in his eyes.

"Nate." She whispered his name. It was all she could manage in the intensity of the moment. Her pulse quickened as his hand slid up her arm, leaving a trail of tingling warmth in its wake.

He didn't respond with words. Instead, he leaned in, his lips brushing against hers in the gentlest of kisses. The touch was feather-light, yet it sent a jolt of electricity through her, igniting a fire that burned deep within her. Mary curled her hands into the fabric of his shirt as she pressed herself closer to him.

Nate cradled the back of her head, tangling his fingers in her hair as the kiss deepened. His lips were warm and insistent, moving against hers with a passion that left her breathless. The world around them faded away, leaving only the two of them, wrapped in each other's embrace as the ship gently rocked beneath their feet.

Mary melted into him, her senses overwhelmed by the taste of salt on his lips, the scent of the sea mingling with the warmth of his skin. The sun caressed her cheeks, but it was Nate's touch that set her skin aflame. Every part of her was attuned to him, to the strength in his arms, the way his body fit perfectly against hers, the way his kiss made her feel as if she were floating on air.

When he finally pulled back, they were both breathless, their foreheads resting against each other as they caught their breath. Nate's eyes were dark with desire, his voice husky. "Mary... I need you."

Her heart skipped a beat at the raw emotion in his words, and an answering heat flared up inside her. "Then take me, Nate," she whispered back, her voice trembling with need. "I'm yours."

Nate's gaze locked onto hers and he scooped her into his arms. Mary let out a soft gasp of surprise, followed by a laugh that was quickly silenced by another kiss, this one even more urgent and consuming.

He told the cabin boy to make sure they weren't disturbed and carried her below deck to their private cabin, a space that he'd had transformed into a haven of luxury and comfort for their journey. A large bed draped in fine linens awaited them, and the soft glow of lanterns cast a warm, intimate light over the room. The door to the cabin closed and locked softly behind them, and in that moment, nothing else mattered. The ship, the island, the vast ocean beyond—it all faded into insignificance as Nate's lips found hers again.

He tenderly set her down on the edge of the bed.

Mary tugged off her bonnet and cast it onto the armchair. "Too many clothes." She gestured between them.

He lifted his brow, pulled at the ties of his shirt, yanked it over his head, and tossed it aside without ceremony.

Mary laughed and allowed herself to stare for a few moments. A flush of warmth crept up her neck. His skin, tanned and smooth, stretched over the hard planes of muscle, each one defined and strong. She loved the way his skin glowed in the soft light. There was something raw and untamed about seeing him like this, stripped of the formal layers society demanded, exposed and yet somehow even more powerful in his simplicity.

A forbidden pleasure, she felt an almost giddy thrill, knowing this was hers alone to admire. No one else would ever know the beauty of him like this, the way his chest rose and fell with each steady breath, the strength that radiated from him.

But her own attire remained, and though she'd chosen a simple linen dress for their island visit, the small laces at the back were conspiring against her.

Nate stepped forward and deftly undid the ties of her dress, his hands warm as they brushed against her waist. As the laces loosened, he pressed a kiss to her collarbone. She shivered in response, her breath hitching as the gown slipped from her shoulders, revealing the soft muslin chemise beneath.

With a teasing grin, Nate made quick work of his breeches, leaving him in nothing but his drawers, his muscles rippling with each movement. "I'm way ahead of you." He teased her as she struggled to free herself from the last of her layers.

She shook her head in mock frustration as she kicked off her slippers. Beneath her gown, she wore the standard underpinnings. A soft chemise, a pair of stays that laced up the front, and stockings held up by garters. She fumbled with the laces of her stays, laughing softly at the contrast between their haste and the delicate layers that kept them apart.

Nate's fingers were quicker than hers, unlacing her stays with ease as he knelt before her, pressing another kiss to the exposed skin just above the hem of her chemise. Her pulse quickened, and the air between them crackled with anticipation. "I'll never understand how you manage all these laces." The teasing note in his voice was replaced with something more heated.

"Years of practice." She stepped out of her stockings and stood nervously before him, as naked as the day she was born. He stood and stared at her as if in a daze. A few seconds passed, so she undid the buttons on his cotton drawers and helped them down his hips. Now there was nothing between them but the soft glow of the lanterns and the thrum of desire that filled the space.

He lowered her gently on the bed, his body hovering over hers, his eyes dark with hunger. "You're so beautiful," he breathed against her ear, sending shivers down her spine.

With infinite tenderness, he kissed her forehead, then her cheeks, then down her jawline, until he reached the hollow of her neck. Nate's lips trailed down her neck to her collarbone, then lower still, eliciting gasps and moans in a language she hadn't known existed until their wedding night. Goosebumps erupted like wildfire across her skin.

He stopped his gentle torture. "Tell me if..."

She reached up and cradled his face in her hands, pulling him back to look into his eyes. "Nate... I'm yours." Her words were a whispered vow.

He nodded once and gripped her hip as he lowered himself over her. Mary arched into him, need and desire coursing through every fibre of her being. His touch was addictive, igniting a fire she'd never known could exist within her. They knew every inch of each other's bodies now, yet each touch still held the same sense of discovery and wonder that had been there on their wedding night.

Their bodies fit together like two pieces of a puzzle longing to be whole, their heartbeats thudding in unison as they moved in the hypnotic rhythm of lovers. The past and the future faded away, leaving only the two of them, lost in each other's arms. Mary closed her eyes and gave herself over to the sensations crashing over her, the heat of his hands, his skin slick against hers, his every touch igniting a fire within her that burned brighter with each passing moment.

A sound escaped her lips, half moan, half sigh as she clung to him. Her world narrowed to the feel of him, to the way their breath mingled as they raced towards the precipice together. And when it finally came, it was like leaping off the side of a cliff. Mary shattered into a million pieces. She cried out his name like it was a sacred mantra, lost in the ecstasy of their union, a breathtaking freefall into oblivion, where nothing else mattered but the crash of their hearts and the knowledge that they were together.

Later, as they lay entwined in a tangle of sheets, breathless, Mary couldn't remember a time when she had ever felt more content.

Wrapped in Nate's arms, she pressed a kiss to his neck. "I'm never letting you go, Lord Everhart."

He cradled her cheek. "That's just as well, as I will never leave your side, Lady Everhart."

Mary smiled knowingly. This Lord and Lady Everhart were destined to spend eternity together.